AMULET BOOKS
NEW YORK

A NOVEL BY

Tucker Shaw

PUBLISHER'S NOTE: This is a work of fiction. Names, characters, places, and incidents are either the product of the author's imagination or are used fictitiously, and any resemblance to actual persons, living or dead, business establishments, events, or locales is entirely coincidental.

Library of Congress Cataloging-in-Publication Data

Shaw, Tucker.
The girls / by Tucker Shaw.
p. cm.
Summary: Inspired by Clare Boothe Luce's *The Women*, a group of high schoolers at the Maroon Bells School for Girls in Aspen, Colorado, experience bonding, jealousy, competition, and fighting over boys as they make decisions about their lives.
ISBN 978-0-8109-8348-9 (alk. paper)
[1. Interpersonal relations—Fiction. 2. Conduct of life—Fiction. 3. Friendship—Fiction. 4. Jealousy—Fiction. 5. High schools—Fiction. 6. Schools—Fiction. 7. Aspen (Colo.)—Fiction.] I. Luce, Clare Boothe, 1903–1987. Women. II. Title.

PZ7.S53445Gi 2009
[Fic]—dc22
2008025576

Text copyright © 2009 Tucker Shaw
Book design by Maria T. Middleton

Printed and bound in U.S.A.
10 9 8 7 6 5 4 3 2 1

Amulet Books are available at special discounts when purchased in quantity for premiums and promotions as well as fundraising or educational use. Special editions can also be created to specification. For details, contact specialmarkets@hnabooks.com or the address below.

HNA
harry n. abrams, inc.
a subsidiary of La Martinière Groupe
115 West 18th Street
New York, NY 10011
www.hnabooks.com

For A,
which stands for *adore*.

PROLOGUE

Mary Moorhead became my best friend the day I arrived at Maroon Bells School for Girls in Aspen, Colorado, last September.

Normally Mom would have driven me, but she'd gotten into a fight with her most recent ex-husband, George, last night, and he ended up taking the Subaru. I thought that after the divorce he would be out of the picture but what do I know about relationships.

So instead, it had taken me six hours and two bus transfers to get there from Denver, and then ten minutes to lug my three overstuffed duffel bags up the two flights of stairs and across the wood-planked hallway floors to my assigned dorm room in Crawford Hall. The door was open when I got there.

A girl stood with her back to me in front of a floor-to-ceiling framed photograph of the Venus de Milo. You know, that ancient Greek statue that's so famous? The half-naked one with no arms and big boobs. The framed photograph, at least eight feet tall, was stark. It only revealed the statue against a white background. The frame leaned against the wall directly opposite the doorway.

The girl had a roll of paper towels in one hand and a bottle of Windex in the other.

She was talking. "At first, I thought it was a black-and-white picture. But look." She leaned in, practically pressing her nose against the glass. "When you get really close, you see the color: gray and green and brown streaks and shadows in the marble. There's a pattern to them. My boyfriend, Stephen, showed me that."

She stepped back and squirted the glass with Windex, still not turning around. She was barefoot, in faded jeans and a chocolate brown V-neck.

"You know, it really should be called the Aphrodite of Melos, not Venus de Milo," said the girl. "They're pretty much the same person, I mean, they're pretty much the same *goddess*. The goddess of love. Most people call her Venus, like the Romans. But the Greeks called her Aphrodite and this is a Greek statue, so, I'm just saying. Her name should be

Aphrodite of Melos." She swept her paper towel across the glass with a squeak. "It's the only print of this photograph in the world."

I slowly lowered my bags to the floor.

"My boyfriend gave it to me," she said.

The girl gave a final swipe, then spun around, tossing her honey blond bangs out of her face and shaking her head. "I know, I'm crazy. I'm sorry. I just love this picture. You must be Peggy Nakamura." She held out her hand. "I'm Mary. Welcome to MBSG."

I took Mary's hand and shook it. A really sparkly bracelet peeked out from the sleeve of her V-neck. I wondered if they were diamonds in it. Probably. This was Aspen. "Hi," I said. "I, um. Nice to meet you." I looked at the floor, or more precisely, at my Pumas.

"Pumas!" Mary said. "Clydes? I love them."

"Thanks," I said, embarrassed by how dusty they were. I'd had this pair of old-school Puma Clydes for just a few months, but I wore them every day. "They're old, but . . ." I shrugged and reached up to pull my ponytail tight. I remember wondering, at that moment, why I hadn't gotten a haircut before leaving Denver. It was halfway down my back, and I had split ends.

"Don't worry," Mary said. "You'll be fine here. Venus, I

mean Aphrodite, is on your side." She blew her bangs out of her face and smiled. "And I'm your friend now." It was a soft soul-smile, the real kind.

My granny used to tell me about different kinds of smiles. *Margaret*, she said, *they say the eyes are the window to the soul, but it is the smile that tells the truth.* I hadn't heard her voice since she died last spring, but I could remember exactly the slow, deliberate way she talked. *A soul-smile cannot be faked.*

Right away, I trusted Mary's smile. But it's what she said next that really made me decide to like her.

"Want to go get a latte?"

That was five months ago, the first day of my junior year at Maroon Bells School for Girls in Aspen, Colorado.

Sunday

1

The Subaru was back, so Mom
drove me to my second semester. It was about ten when Mom
dropped me off after the long drive from Denver, which, if
you're doing the math, started at about six thirty this morning.
After spending the entire drive asleep in the backseat
dreaming about the breakfast we never stopped for, I heard
her ask if I wanted her to drop me off at the Timberline coffee
shop on Hunter Street, which everyone around here calls the
Timberlake, which says a lot about the people around here. I
said sure. I'd get a coffee and a croissant then walk the half-
mile to campus. It was sunny out. It was warm enough.

She pulled over in front of the Timberlake and kissed me
on the cheek. "Bye," she said.

We didn't make a big deal about saying good-bye, because I don't think she wanted to. We'd had a good winter break, baking and eating and watching two movies a day from Netflix. I guess it was easier for her to pretend she was just dropping me off at the coffee shop down the street for a few minutes, instead of at school, three hours away, for a whole semester.

I slipped my sunglasses on and stepped out of the car. A gust of frozen wind caught my scarf, which I grabbed in midair just as it blew off my neck. Maybe it wasn't so warm. Mom called days like this "fake out" days—blazingly sunny and hot in the car, but breathlessly frigid as soon as you opened the door.

It was tough to keep my balance in the wind as I struggled with my effing nine-thousand-pound duffel bag through the eight inches of fresh snow to the Timberlake. I probably should have been wearing boots, not my Pumas. I pulled open the glass door, which took two hands and a grunt, but before I could step through the threshold, this shiny, skinny, sleek, black-clad figure in ridiculously high stiletto boots stepped through in front of me like a spider.

"Thanks, Penny," she said.

"It's *Peggy*," I said.

"Oh," she said. "Whatever." Sylvia Fowler pushed past

and strode toward the counter, black stilettos clacking with each step.

I stood in the doorway, stuck, tangled in my scarf and duffel strap, watching her spidery walk.

"Can you close the door?" asked the woman sitting at the nearest two-top. She was glare-smiling at me. Granny taught me that one, too. A baby, whose head was exposed above a sagging cashmere blanket wrapped around her torso, wriggled in her arms. "It's freezing out there. My Paulette is getting cold." She pulled the ivory blanket around herself, which left her baby's feet uncovered. I realized she was nursing.

"Sure," I said. "Here." I straightened my duffel strap, then reached over and tucked the blanket around Paulette's feet. The woman didn't say thank you.

I sighed and got in line behind Sylvia. I eyed the pastry case, making sure, of course, that there was a plain croissant. I like my croissants plain. No chocolate. No Asiago cheese and asparagus. No rosemary. Just a plain, gooshy, buttery, soft croissant, barely warm, with a little bit of extra butter on top. What can I say, I'm a butter freak.

No one understood this in Aspen. It's funny. Even though Denver was only three hours away (two and three-quarters if I'm driving), I never came here when I was a kid. Ever. I didn't even know anyone who did. Aspen was a totally different world, a fancy place for out-of-staters, celebrities, and billionaires. It was for people who had nothing to do with the laid-back Colorado I knew. Part of me was glad I didn't fit in.

"Latte, Andrea," Sylvia said at the barista, whose name was Amber, which Sylvia knew. She pushed her black wraparound sunglasses up onto her black patent-leather hair, pulled back into a crazy-tight chignon.

Chignon. Now there was a word I never knew before I got to Aspen. Or needed.

"A big one," Sylvia said, to elaborate. She licked one of her black-gloved fingers and reached back to spit-shine the heel of her left boot.

You have to hand it to Sylvia. She was committed to being Sylvia. And that meant wearing black. In the sea of blond shearling and gray chinchilla and white quilted nylon that is the Timberlake, that is any coffee shop in Aspen for that matter, Sylvia was always the only one in black, hair included. Knee-high boots, thick black tights, thigh-length wrap coat, bulky cashmere scarf, driving gloves, mascara—all black, deep black, sleek against her icy white skin. The only things not black or white were her lips, thickly coated in the richest, shiniest ruby red lipstick.

But despite how intimidating the package may have

seemed, Sylvia was, somehow, harmless. An insult from Sylvia almost didn't count because it was never about you. It was about Sylvia being Sylvia.

I marveled another moment at her boots, which probably cost more than the yearly tuition to MBSG. I wondered which she valued more.

Amber started packing espresso for Sylvia's latte. I watched Sylvia narrow her eyes and lock them into the back of Amber's head. Sylvia knew that Amber always had fresh gossip. She made lattes for everyone. *Everyone.* And she made sure everyone got a shot of gossip with their coffee.

"So," said Sylvia, licking her red lips. "Was winter break boring, or what?" She dug through the suitcase-size, buckle-heavy (black, duh) leather handbag hanging from her forearm.

Amber wrenched the espresso lever into the press, refastened her curly ponytail, and shook her head. "Are you kidding?"

Sylvia pursed her lips, forcing the sharp corners of her mouth up into the tiniest of smiles. "Oh?" She pulled a compact out of her bag, faking indifference.

Amber set down a paper cup and inhaled deeply. "It was insane. Mariah Carey was in three times. I want to hate her, but I can't. It would be too easy. I mean, even the girl's parkas show cleavage. That's serious commitment. You could tell she was annoyed that there weren't any paparazzi the first time she was in. Kate Hudson was here with Ryder. You know, her son? He kind of looks like a girl with all that long hair. That's what I want, a boy who looks like a girl. It would be perfect." Amber carefully poured Sylvia's latte, then grabbed for a plastic sip-top, but the pile of sip-tops were all stuck together. She dug her pink-polished fingernail into the one on top, trying to separate them, but the stack slipped out of her grasp and fell, sending a dozen sip-tops sliding across the counter. Yet Amber was still trying to separate the two at the top. It was so awkward that I wanted to just reach over and push her out of the way and do it myself.

"Actually, I want two. Two girl-boys. That would be perfect. She was here with some guy. At first I thought it was Lance Armstrong but this guy was fatter. Maybe it was her brother, Oliver. But I wouldn't really recognize him anyway. Oh, and Fergie was supposedly in here, too, but I wasn't working that day." She finally separated the sip-top she wanted and started to cap Sylvia's latte.

"No top," Sylvia said, waving Amber and her hard-won sip-top away. Staring intently into her compact, Sylvia raised her hand to smooth her Plasticine hair. She stopped short of actually touching it.

"Anyway, who else was here?" Amber said. "Let's see, Heidi Klum, Maria Sharapova, oh, and that guy from *Top Chef* . . . oh, and you probably heard about that whole thing with Stephen Haines-Durant. You know him. His father owns the Durant Hotel up the street. Anyway, he's supposed to be going out with Mary Moorhead, right? Perfect couple, right? Richest guy in Aspen and richest girl at Maroon Bells? Anyway, he's been hooking up with some girl who works at Mod."

I froze. Did I really hear what I just heard? Stephen Haines? Mary's boyfriend? My roommate Mary's boyfriend? No effing way. It couldn't be. Amber got it wrong. Stephen was in love with Mary. He'd never fool around on her. Would he?

Amber was still talking. "Yeah, she works at Mod. Do you know Mod? That jeans shop over on Cooper?"

Sylvia's black leather collar bunched at her neck. "I don't shop there." She snapped her compact shut with a *clack*, like she was punctuating her point. "Never have."

It was like Amber didn't even hear her. "I think her name is, like, Topaz or something. Like some kind of jewelry. You know, like Sapphire, maybe, or Diamond."

"Or *Amber*?" Sylvia cocked an eyebrow and rolled her eyes at the same time. I swear she had double-jointed eyebrows. She sipped her latte, leaving red lipstick residue on the foam. It didn't look like blood, not *exactly*.

"No," said Amber, not getting the joke. "What was it, Ruby? Pearl? Oh yes, Crystal! That's it. Crystal." She wiped her hands on her apron and shook her head. "Can you believe it? Stephen Haines with some girl from down valley."

Half of me wanted to turn around and get out of there. Like, if I didn't hear it, if I didn't know about it, then it wouldn't be true. Thanks to Mary, I was now friends with Stephen. He was the kind of guy I never thought actually existed. You wanted to hate him, but you couldn't: model-gorgeous with gray green eyes, absurdly rich . . . but he was also funny, smart, even heroic. His jeans, faded to that fuzzy line halfway between midnight and indigo, weren't adorned with stitching or logos; just plain, worn, perfect. Stephen was the youngest, and blondest, member of the Aspen Ski Patrol, a role he seemed born for; after all, his family had been living and skiing in Aspen for, like, three generations or something. They'd owned the oldest and most expensive hotel in town, the Durant, a national historic landmark. In fact, he and Mary met when she broke her collarbone skiing last year and he rescued her. (That's the heroic part.)

And Mary, the female version of Stephen, honey blond and rich and perfect and wholesome, totally hateable if only she wasn't so cool. She was a New York City girl, Upper East Sider from the kind of old-money family that you don't read about in the gossip columns, the kind of family so drenched with money it makes those gossip-girlie socialites seem desperate and crass. There was nothing flashy about her, but all her sweaters were cashmere, all her equestrian boots custom-made. Unlike Sylvia, Mary never made the mistake of believing that anyone else cared about her wealth, and she never talked about it.

They really were the perfect couple. And ever since I'd known them, they had been attached at the hip.

Half of me knew for sure: Stephen would never cheat on Mary. This couldn't be true.

But the other half of me knew I had to keep listening to Amber. I really needed that croissant now. It would help me think.

"Down valley?" Sylvia asked. She was trying so hard to act bored.

"I *know*!" Amber squawked. "Glenwood Springs, I think."

"Hmm?" said Sylvia. "Glenwood what? Where's that?"

Sylvia knew exactly where Glenwood Springs was. It was a half hour away and by far the biggest town around here. Unless you flew out of Aspen by jet, it was just about impossible to leave the valley without going through Glenwood Springs. (Unless Independence Pass was open, and that was only in the summer.) Glenwood was too working-class for people like Sylvia. But since it's not politically correct to be a snob about it, she just pretended she'd never heard of it. Which in a way, was even worse.

"Well, it's not here," Amber said. "But that didn't stop the Prince of Aspen from hooking up with her."

"He's a prince, all right." Sylvia ran a finger across her waxy eyebrow.

Amber started restacking the sip-tops. "I *know*!" she squawked again. "Guys are all the same. You can't trust any of them, not even the perfect ones. They always end up cheating sooner or later. We'd be better off without them at all. I was watching *Tyra* the other day, and she was interviewing this woman who'd decided to go celibate, but she seemed so miserable. And it was weird because right after that there was an episode of *Snapped*. Do you know *Snapped*? It's a show about women who can't take it anymore and kill their husbands. Anyway, the woman on *Tyra* and the woman on *Snapped* seemed so similar, like they had something in common. It was weird." Amber leaned across the counter and lowered her voice. "Poor Mary," she said. "She's so nice. And pretty. She's going to be devastated if she finds out."

Sylvia stared at Amber for a second. "Devastated," she said coldly.

"I *know*!" Amber said, a little less squawkish.

Sylvia took a gulp of her still-searing-hot latte, a big one, the kind of gulp that would burn a normal mouth, but not Sylvia's, then dramatically dropped the mostly unfinished cup into the trash can next to the counter. She slid her sunglasses back over her eyes and dropped a crumpled twenty-dollar bill on the counter. "I need a ten-dollar gift card."

Amber started punching buttons on the cash register. "Fourteen twenty-five," she said. "And what is that lipstick you have on? It's so red."

"*Jungle red*," said Sylvia. "It's from Dubai. You can't get it here."

2

I left the Timberlake without even
ordering a coffee or a croissant. Which meant that I'd have a
headache for the rest of the day. Which meant the noise in the
crowded MBSG student union was even more annoying than
usual. Giggles and hand slaps and squeals echoed through
the elbow-to-elbow room, rising to the high ceilings before
consolidating and raining back onto the floor.

"Hiiiiiii!"

"Omigod hiiiiiii!"

"Hi!!!! You're soooooooooo tan!"

"No, you!"

I swear, all-girl boarding school student unions, especially on the first day after winter vacation, ought to come

with an effing health warning: The decibel levels reached by the dozens of simultaneous, piggybacked squeals are unmatched outside rocket launches and death metal concerts, and probably could cause permanent eardrum damage.

Actually, I don't know if I can really say that with such confidence. Maroon Bells School for Girls was the first and only all-girls boarding school I'd ever set foot in. I would have never come here at all, except last spring I kind of lost my mind and applied and then got accepted and sort of had no choice but to come.

See, I was really going through it at home. I lost my best friend, Jane, when she hooked up with my boyfriend, Booth, whose real name was Clarence but he wanted to be called Booth, which should have been a red flag, I guess. And Mom kicked out George, who was my third stepfather and to be honest the first one who didn't give me the creeps. So I stopped talking to her. And then I got accepted to this six-week cooking program at the Italian Culinary Institute in New York, only I couldn't afford to go. And then George came back, then he left again. Then I made the mistake of making out with Booth, who was now my ex, after some stupid spring dance I didn't even want to go to in the first place, after which he told everyone at school, which totally made me the school ho which I totally wasn't. Oh, and Granny died.

I don't know, it was like drama overload.

I decided the only way out was out, so I went online and googled "boarding school." The first hit was Maroon Bells School for Girls. The Web site was beautiful, packed with pictures of a perfect, easygoing world full of girls horseback riding, shopping, and snowboarding.

Snowboarding, I thought. That sounds fun. And no boys to screw things up.

It seemed perfect. I could leave my annoying life and start a new one, a perfect new one, a clean, easy slate, just like in the pictures on the MBSG Web site. Later I'd realize that many of the perfect pictures were of Mary, which made sense. Her life seemed just about perfect. Until a few minutes ago, anyway.

I couldn't resist the perfect, so I applied. Right then and there. I used my mother's credit card for the application fee.

I kind of regretted it the next morning, but I knew I wouldn't get in anyway and I'd just pay Mom back.

Except, I *did* get accepted. And they offered me a full scholarship. It was weird, because by the time I found out, Mom and I had made up about the George thing, and I wasn't sure if I really wanted to go anymore. But everyone said I should go. It was such a good opportunity. *It will give you an advantage*, they said. *And you can learn to snowboard!*

And so, here I was. Three hours and a million miles away

from my public-school, boy-drama-filled life in Denver, halfway through a school year in a foreign world, stuffed with dozens of shrieking girls in really expensive outfits into the sprawling MBSG student union with its football-field-size Persian rug, soaring atrium windows, and exposed aspen-wood beams that lined the ceiling like ivory ribs. I knew my way around this perfect world by now. I'd even learned to snowboard.

But I was choking on Amber's gossip, afraid to puncture Mary's picture-perfect life. I didn't know what to do with the news. Should I tell her? Not tell her?

I didn't want to talk to anyone. But to get to my room in Crawford Hall, I had to power through the shrieking melee. My plan—to keep my sunglasses on and therefore go entirely unnoticed—unraveled only a few steps into the crowd.

"Hi, Peggy," said Ginny, who had three tiny braids in her otherwise frizzed-out hair. "I'm so tired. I just got back from Cabo. Do you know how long it takes to get back from Cabo? It takes forever, that's how long." She lurched forward, pushed from behind by a crush of girls. "Ouch! Have you seen Mary?"

I shook my head, swatted an errant blond ponytail out of my face, and pressed on. I decided to skip the mailboxes and head straight for the back exit, which led directly to Crawford.

"Have you seen Mary?" asked Claire, who was sitting on

her suitcase and flipping through a stack of mail, most of which looked like credit card applications. "I have to ask her something."

"Nope," I said, and kept moving, pushing a Louis Vuitton rolling trunk aside with my Puma.

"Hi!" squawked Anita, springing into my path like a howler monkey. "Is Mary back yet?" She didn't look me in the eye when she asked, so I didn't reach out to catch her cardigan when it slipped off her shoulders and onto the floor. "My sweater!" she squeaked, but it was too late; Aileen Chambers's Ugg stepped squarely on the sleeve, leaving a slushy mark.

"I don't know where Mary is," I said. And then, under my breath, "Nice to see you, too." I didn't stop moving.

"Peggy," said Ms. Shearer, in her trendy plaid skirt and fisherman's sweater. "Did you sign up for newspaper? We need a restaurant critic and I thought of you." It was impossible to tell her age. Her old-fashioned haircut might have been retro, or it might have been real. "Think about it."

"I will," I said, happy to have my sunglasses on so she couldn't see my eyes roll. I had no intention of signing up for newspaper. It was called *The Belltower*, for one thing, and besides, everyone on the staff looked like an effing Olsen twin.

"Well, have you seen Mary?" Ms. Shearer asked. "I want her to be the campus editor."

I shook my head and pressed through the crowd, out the back door, and into Crawford Hall. Once in my room, I locked the door and dropped my duffel on the bed.

Venus, I mean Aphrodite, was looking at me. "What?" I asked, aloud. "What do you want? No, I don't know where Mary is." The sun was pouring in our western-facing window (which sounds more glamorous than it is, because it looks out onto an alley, which we share with the Durant Hotel. The only view we have is a Dumpster, really, and the occasional cute waiter). I pulled the curtain shut.

Whenever I have too much on my mind, I make up things I want to eat. I've done it ever since I was little. The first time I remember doing it was in traffic. I was strapped into the backseat, and it was hot, and the sun was beating down through the backseat window onto my legs, and my seatbelt was digging into a bruise on my shoulder, and my mother was ignoring me, like she'd forgotten I was there, and she was singing so loud, some song I recognized at the time but now couldn't remember, and I just remember feeling so trapped. And there was no way out of this car, out of this traffic jam, out of this heat. And so, I started to cook in my head.

Maple syrup sandwiches. Hamburger nuggets. Ice-cream pie. Chocolate-covered chocolate.

Later, when I got older, the dishes got more complicated.

Three-cheese fondue with potato croquettes. Chilled pea soup with sour cream and tarragon. Grilled peaches with berry granita.

A stack of papers from last semester sat on my desk. Dead weight. I pushed it onto the floor, sending sheets flying in every direction. I threw my sunglasses on the desk and collapsed in my folding chair.

So my best friend's boyfriend was cheating on her.

What was I supposed to do now?

Lobster-claw salad on twice-buttered griddle rolls. Southern-fried chicken with Cajun-spiced cornbread. Peach upside-down cake with butterscotch pudding.

3

What I did was go to work.

Chef Jackie was on her stool in front of her laptop by the back delivery door when I arrived in the kitchen at Reno. "Hi," she said, without looking up. "Onions." She gestured across the counter to a basket of yellow onions, probably eight pounds' worth.

"Soup?" I asked.

"Mmm-hmm," she mumbled. I realized then that she was on the phone. "Really? No monkfish? I specifically asked for five tails this morning, and your guy only brought me one. What gives?"

I hung up my parka and striped scarf on the hook by the employee's bathroom and tied an apron around my waist, looping the strings around and into a bow in the front. I picked my eight-inch chef's knife from the block (we didn't share knives at Reno, it was a Chef Jackie thing) and started sharpening it against the honer.

Reno's kitchen was really tiny; any more than three people in there and you were just as likely to slice off someone else's finger as your own. The main prep counter, just five feet long, was a single piece of wood cut from a really big tree. Chef Jackie had it sanded down three or four times a year. She told me it was fifty years old. And at its far end it fell off into a deep prep sink. Above it was a long, narrow pass-through into the dining room, where servers out front would pick up dishes to deliver to diners.

Most of the servers were classmates of mine. Reno was a new restaurant, and even though it was written up in the *Aspen Chronicle* last fall as the Best New Restaurant in Pitkin County, Jackie still wasn't making that much money. And MBSC girls came cheap. Some worked for extra cash, some just because Reno was this year's hot restaurant, and if your goal for the season was to meet a movie star, Reno was the place to do it.

I was the only one at Reno on work-study, and the only one working in the kitchen instead of out front. Mary got me the job. She took Chef Jackie a Tupperware full of some macaroni and cheese I made on our hot plate last fall, which at first pissed me off because I didn't think it was that good, but that afternoon Chef Jackie called me and asked if I wanted a job. I started telling her about my experience working in my granny's diner but she just interrupted me. "Can you chop onions?" I said yes, and she said, "Get all the prep work done by six, stay nearby but out of the way during service, and above all, don't wait to ask for help. Eight-fifty an hour. When can you start?"

Since then, three afternoons a week, it was just me and Jackie in the kitchen. She on the laptop, me chopping something.

"Phelps, don't lie to me. I happen to know that D19 and Matsuhisa both got monkfish this morning. How come you didn't short them?" She picked at the knee-hole in her jeans, whisking away the exposed threads.

I grabbed an onion. I placed my heavy knife on top of it and, to test the sharpness of my blade, applied just a hit of pressure to the knife. It slid straight through the onion and into the countertop with a *thwack*. Perfect. Its pungent aroma hit my nose and, almost immediately, my eyes teared up. These were some serious weepers.

"I want six monkfish tomorrow, Phelps. No screwing around." She slapped shut her cell.

Chef Jackie pushed up the sleeves of her thermal T-shirt and tucked her hair behind a headband she'd fashioned from a white bandanna. She stared at me for a moment, squinting at my eyes. Then she turned back to her laptop. "What's wrong, Peg?"

I hated it when she called me Peg. "Nothing," I said. "It's the onions." *Chop*.

"Are you sure?" said Chef Jackie.

I didn't answer. I looked at the leather wrist cuff snapped over her forearm and wondered how old Chef Jackie was. I didn't know. I don't think anyone did. All I know was that she graduated from MBSG back in the '90s. She was on the ski team, a star apparently, but she broke her leg senior year so couldn't compete after that. She never talked about it. After high school, when everyone else went off to Wellesley and Columbia, she went to Italy to work in a kitchen in Rome. She stayed ten years. When she got back to Aspen a year ago, she was alone, but there was a rumor that she had a husband back in Italy. But she never talked about that either.

"Chef?" I said. "Have you seen Mary?" *Chop*.

"No. Why?"

"Just wondering." *Chop*. I raised my arms and dabbed my eyes on my shoulders.

I scraped the onions I'd chopped so far, about eight cups'

worth, into the prep bowl. Chef Jackie grabbed my shoulders and squeezed past me to yank open the freezer-closet, which burped out a cloud of frozen air around her. For a second, through my tears and the cloud, she looked like a rock star.

"We're low on ice cream," she said. "And we're doing apple and pear crumble tonight. I better call Russell for more ice cream. Which is the last thing I can afford right now. And why do we have all these extra eggs? What am I supposed to do with them?"

"Chef?" *Chop. Chop.*

"Yeah?"

"Do you have a boyfriend?" I'm not sure, still, why I asked her that question. With everything that was on my mind, it came out of nowhere. *Chop.*

Chef Jackie laughed. "Uh, no," she said. "Not really." She slammed the freezer door.

"What do you mean, not really?" *Chop.*

"Well, do you mean like a boyfriend-boyfriend?" Jackie squeezed behind me and plopped back down in front of her laptop. "We need more pork loin, too. That's been selling well."

"What's a boyfriend-boyfriend?" *Chop. Scrape.*

"You know," she said. "Like a boyfriend you really like. Like Mary, and what's his name."

"Stephen?"

"Yes, Stephen Haines. Durant. Haines-Durant. Whatever his name is. That's a boyfriend-boyfriend."

"Oh," I said. *Chop.*

"You can tell she likes him," Chef Jackie said. "It's in the eyes."

Chop. Or the smile, I thought. *The smile tells the truth.*

"You could do a sabayon," I said. "Instead of the ice cream."

"What?" Jackie said.

"A sabayon. For the crumble. You have all those extra eggs. It would be easy. Just egg yolks and sugar and vanilla. Or wine."

"Who's going to stand there whisking it all night?" Jackie said. "I can't make a sabayon ahead of time and leave it sitting around. It will break."

"I can," I said. "I can do it."

Jackie looked over at me from her laptop. She studied me for a second, then smiled, slowly. "Yes, I guess you can," she said. "Sabayon it is."

"Is she on the schedule tonight?" I asked, meaning Mary, hoping that she wasn't. I still didn't know what to do yet, with this news in my head. Which was just gossip really. Right? It wasn't really news. I mean, I can't go around spreading gossip. It wouldn't be right.

Besides, maybe she'd already heard. Maybe it was just another story that Amber screwed up. Maybe Mary and Stephen had already had a laugh about how silly it was.

Or maybe not. Maybe Amber's story was true. Maybe Stephen hooked up with another girl. If it was true, my friend's, no, my *best* friend's heart would break. In half. And I wouldn't know how to put it back together.

"Is she?" *Chop*. "On the schedule?" *Scrape*. I noticed that I'd stopped crying.

"I don't know," Chef Jackie said. She grabbed her mouse and started clicking. "Ask Edie."

4

I pushed through the kitchen door
and into Reno's tiny dining room. There were eleven tables,
five four-tops and six two-tops, lined up along the walls,
which were wood-paneled up to chair height, then exposed
brick above. The room was homey, cabinlike, and kind of
rickety, but also sort of cool. I loved the modern teak sconces
above each table, which sent a drape of soft light down the
brick. Six massive, beautiful drawings of vegetables, in lines
of green and charcoal, framed the front window, which
looked out onto Cooper Avenue.

That's where Edie was. Up by the window.

Edie was the hostess at Reno. She was also the first girl at
MBSG to turn eighteen, so she got to vote in the presidential

election, which she never shuts up about, and which also really annoys me because she's the kind of girl who would submit a write-in vote for Perez Hilton.

Edie didn't get to work as early as I did, but she was usually there every night during dinner. Chef Jackie insisted that she call and reconfirm all the reservations for the night. She almost never moved from her perch at the chest-high podium just inside the mudroom, which was blocked off with velvet curtains to keep out the cold. Come to think of it, Edie had to stand on a box to see over the podium, so I guess the chest-high thing depends on how tall you are. She could see the whole dining room from there, from the kitchen door and pass-through in the back, to the waiters' station where servers' silverware, ice water, and salt and pepper shakers sat, to the two doors, marked "M" and "W" in the alcove across from the entrance. On busy nights, which was pretty much every night lately, Edie would stick another two-top by the front window, but no one liked sitting there, because it was drafty.

Edie was hanging up the house phone when I reached her podium. "Peggy," she said. She was wide-eyed, unblinking, chewing on a flyaway chunk of her burgundy faux-goth bob, which matched the wide belt around the waist of her white French-cuffed shirtdress. Black tights, thick, and low boots.

"Peggy. That was Amber. Oh, my god. She told me. About Mary. Did you hear? Did she tell you? Oh. My. God. Peggy. Amber. Mary. Too much." She had a hybrid smile, delight and panic.

I stared into her anime eyes and lied. "I don't know what you're talking about." I knew she didn't believe me, but it was the most obvious way I could think of to say, I already know. Do us both a favor and shut up. "Is Mary on the schedule tonight?"

Edie's eyes got even bigger, then she spit out her hair and grabbed the schedule. "Yes. Mary, Joanie, and Luce." The phone rang. Still staring at me, she reached over and picked it up. "Reno, this is Edie."

I looked at my watch. Mary would be here in less than an hour. What was I going to do?

Turkish lamb kebabs with tomatoes and Urfa peppers.

I turned back toward the kitchen and started chewing on my nail. Abruptly, I changed course and headed for the bathroom. I sat there for a while, chewing my nail and playing through every scenario I could think of. If it was true, and she'd already heard, I would hug her, and she would cry, and I would cry, and the whole semester would suck. If she hadn't already heard, and I didn't tell her, and it turned out to be true, then she would be mad at me for not telling her. Then again, if I did tell her, and it turned out to be not true, she would think I was spreading gossip about her. But if it was true, and I didn't tell her, and she found out later that I knew and didn't tell her, then she would think she couldn't trust me. Then again, if I didn't tell her, and it wasn't true, and she did find out that people were spreading gossip about her, and that I'd heard it and didn't say anything, she would think I didn't trust her. Or something. It all made me dizzy.

I checked my watch. It was almost four o'clock. And I was nowhere near done with prep. Chef Jackie would kill me.

Chiles rellenos with mole sauce. Chocolate torte with caramel-pecan whipped cream.

5

𝓘 spent the next half hour jumping
every time the front door opened, waiting for Mary to arrive.
Where was she? Did she know already? Had she heard? I
thought as soon as I saw her, I'd know.

I heard Mary before I saw her.

Her voice drifted across the pass-through counter, animated and lively. She was yakking about her winter vacation to Edie, who kept trying, and failing, to get a word in. I didn't look up. I wasn't ready to see her smile.

"It was awesome. I mean, awesome. Well, it was wet. But I just love being home for Christmas. Everyone else goes to Switzerland or whatever, but I like being in the city. New York just looks amazing with all the lights. I feel like a tourist, it's *so* fun."

I still didn't look up from my cutting board. But I didn't have to. I could hear it. She didn't know.

"Mary?" Edie nudged. They were approaching the kitchen door.

"And you should see my little brother right now. He is so cute. He has his first girlfriend! And she's a year older than he is!" Mary stood just outside the kitchen door for a moment, still talking. "Can you imagine, a seventh grader from St. David's dating an eighth grader from Nightingale?" she gasped exaggeratedly. "I think they met at a dance. Because, you know, girls and boys are never allowed around each other except at a dance. Oh, Edie," she burst through the swinging door into the kitchen. "The drama!"

"I hate New York," Chef Jackie said, low and aside, to me, but loud enough for Mary to hear.

"Oh, shut up! You do not!" Mary blew her bangs out of her face and threw a small bundle at Chef Jackie, which Jackie easily caught with one hand. "I got you a present. It's an FDNY bandanna. You know, just to throw into the mix." She pointed at Chef Jackie's bandanna. "I figure a girl can never have too many bandannas."

Mary turned to me. "Peggy!" She pushed up her cashmere sleeves and walked over, shaking her finger in the air. She grabbed me by the shoulders, suddenly serious. She crossed her eyebrows. "Why didn't you tell me?" she demanded.

Oh, my god. I looked down, and over to Jackie, and back up to Mary, who was glaring. Did she know? Did she know that I knew? My stomach dropped into my shoes. This was just about the worst case from my worst-case scenario exercise earlier today.

Cinnamon bread pudding. Seared tuna tacos with salsa fresca.

"Um," I said, or stuttered. "I, um. I don't know." And then, figuring I had nothing to lose, I played dumb. "Why didn't I tell you *what*?"

"About your bangs! I didn't know you were going to get bangs over break!" Suddenly her face brightened up. "They look fantastic!" She reached out and ruffled my hair, then leaned in and wrapped her arms around me, in a bear hug. "I missed you!"

"I missed you, too," I said, not really relieved. "Sorry I didn't confer with you about the bangs. It was kind of spur of the moment." Mary let go and started unbuttoning her forest green quilted nylon jacket.

"Well," Mary said as she slipped her jacket over a hook next to mine, "I like them. I think you look great." She held out her hands toward me, as if offering her nails for inspection. "What's on the menu tonight?"

I wiped my hands on a towel, then took her crisp white cuff and started rolling up her sleeves. It was a thing we did, because she was incapable of rolling up her own sleeves without them looking messy and loose and eventually falling into some customer's sauce. And then they'd throw a fit, and Chef Jackie would have to go out and apologize. So we decided that I'd roll up Mary's sleeves before her shift. She also had to wear a skinny black tie, but she did that herself.

I finished the right cuff and moved to the left. "Wow," I said, startled. There, on her wrist, was a shiny, onyx-faced watch, framed with what looked like tiny diamonds set in rows. The band was brushed metal, platinum probably, a masculine band but very slim. I nodded at it. "Nice," I said. "New?"

"It's from Stephen," she said. "It's a Patek Phillippe. There's a boy version, too, so I got it for him. I'll give it to him tonight. Isn't it cute? Our wrists are going to match." She smiled for a moment, then clasped her hand over her watch. "OK, now even *I* am going to gag."

Then, she leaned in and hugged me. "It is so good to see you," she said. "Next year, you are coming to New York to spend Christmas with me. Just think of all the good food you'll get to try!"

I'd never been to New York. Granny was there once, right after World War II. *It was full of smiles, Margaret,* she said. *But with all those lights, it was hard to tell which smiles to trust.*

But I always wanted to go anyway. Everyone says it has the

best food anywhere. I almost got to go last Christmas, when George promised to take me and Mom, but obviously that never happened.

Mary grabbed a tray and put it on the pass-through counter. Humming, she started stacking water glasses on it. She'd tried to secure her hair on top of her head with a barrette, but more of it was loose than pinned, and wisps of hair just fell all across her face and shoulders. But she didn't seem to notice. She was like the anti-Sylvia.

Just then Chef Jackie leaped up from her stool. "It's here!" she shouted. "It's here! I can't believe it. It's here."

Mary and I looked at Chef Jackie. *"What's* here?" Mary said.

"Peg?" Chef Jackie said. Ugh, *Peg.* "I have to run out. I have a surprise for us. I'll be back in an hour." She bolted out the back door.

"OK," I said to the door.

"What was that about?" Mary asked.

"It's a Berkel. It's supposed to be a surprise but I know about it already." I went back to the chicken stock I was supposed to be straining. "It's a meat slicer—a really good one, from Italy. Really expensive. She wanted to surprise me."

"She wanted to surprise you," Mary said. "With a meat slicer."

"Yeah. I guess. So don't tell her I know."

"Um, Peggy?" Mary said. "You are the biggest food nerd I know!"

"Shut up," I said, smiling, knowing it was true and not minding it. "So," I said, changing the subject. "Have you talked to him yet?"

"Who?" Mary went back to humming and glass stacking.

"Stephen!" I said.

"No, not yet," Mary said. "He was supposed to pick me up at the airport, but he texted me that he was stuck at some ski-patrol thing. Probably another training session for CPR or something." She stopped stacking and looked at her watch. "God, I love that boy."

I didn't answer.

"Peggy," she said after a moment. "Can I ask you a question?"

"Sure," I said, not looking up. Just being around her right now made me nervous. I felt like everything I wasn't saying was written on my forehead, and if I looked at Mary too much, she'd see it. "What's up?"

"Have you ever been in love?" she asked. "I mean, *really* in love?"

I paused for a minute, wondering about the *really* part. "I don't know," I said. "No, I guess. Why?"

"I've never felt anything like it," she said. "It's like, so different from a crush. I mean, I'm not obsessed with him, you know? I'm not, like, worried about losing him. And he's never pressured me to, you *know* . . . I trust him. It's so new to me." She stacked one last glass. "He's the first guy I've ever known that I didn't want to completely change."

This was worse than I thought it would be. She definitely hadn't heard the news. I mean, the *gossip*. Which I didn't want to spread.

"Well," I stuttered. "Everyone says he's perfect. Can't improve on that."

"He's not perfect," Mary said. "But I don't want him perfect. I want him, like, I don't know. I want *him—*"

"Just the way he is?" I interrupted, desperate for a window out of this conversation. I rolled my eyes teasingly and pushed her away. She smiled.

Mary kept her cell phone in her back pocket so that when it rang she could jump up and yell, "My butt's ringing!" Which she did right then. Which made me laugh.

OK, so I admit. "My butt's ringing!" isn't all that original, or even all that funny. But something about the fact that Mary said it all the freaking time, every single time her phone rings, which is constantly, makes it funnier. Like, the more you tell the same stupid joke, the funnier it gets.

"It's Stephen's ring." She looked up at me, eyes sparkling, and bit her lower lip.

Another ring, and she answered. "Hey," she said, brightly, then "hey" again, softly. She turned and shuffled out Reno's back door, into the alley. The door slammed behind her.

Duck breast with rhubarb reduction. Lamb medallions with sautéed gnocchi and wild mushrooms. Wilted frisée salad with poached eggs.

I tapped my knife on my cutting board and looked around for something to chop.

7

While Mary was out back, I

practiced the sabayon. Twice. It came out perfect.

8

Twenty minutes after her phone
rang, Mary unlatched the kitchen door and stepped back
inside, shivering. "It's snowing again."

"I should have brought you your coat," I said. She shook
her head. Her lips were pursed, face screwed up quizzically.
"What?" I said.

"That was Stephen."

"I know," I said.

"He's in Glenwood Springs. Still stuck with the ski patrol.
He's not going to be back until late tonight. They're having dinner there. I'm so bummed. I guess he forgot he was supposed
to pick me up this afternoon, but he said he's going to take
me to Matsuhisa tomorrow night. He says he wants to talk."

Glenwood Springs? For ski patrol? That wasn't right. Glenwood Springs is nowhere near a ski mountain. And come to think of it, isn't that where Amber said that Topaz girl was from? "Glenwood Springs?" I asked.

"I know. Strange, huh?" Mary said. "They're probably learning how to set a compound fracture at the hospital there or something." She sat down on the folding chair by the coat hooks and crossed her right leg across her left knee. "My feet are killing me," she said.

"New boots?" I asked.

"Yeah," she said. "And I forgot my sneakers."

"Trade?" I asked. I pointed to my comfy green-and-black Pumas.

"I love you," Mary said. I sat down next to her and we traded shoes. "Where did Chef Jackie say she was going? To get a Perkel?"

"Berkel," I said. "But we don't know that, remember? It's a surprise."

Mary grabbed my apron strings and yanked, untying the bow. "Nerd." She pulled my apron off and tossed it on the counter. "Come on. It's only four forty-five. Jackie's gone for a half hour at least. Let's go get a latte." She grabbed our coats and tossed mine at me. "Besides, you have to tell me about Denver. I want to hear everything! What did you get for Christmas? How is your mom? Did I mention I'm having dinner with Stephen at Matsuhisa tomorrow night?"

"I heard," I said, elbowing her in the ribs as she pushed me through the swinging door.

Mary took my elbow and led me toward the front door. Just as we reached Edie's podium, a blast of cold air, and then Sylvia, swept through the velvet curtains.

I gasped. Oh, no. Sylvia was going to tell Mary. It was going to go down right now. I scrambled through my brain looking for a reason to go back to the kitchen, but Mary clamped down on my elbow. Crap. I don't want to be here for this, I thought. Then I felt bad for thinking that.

"Hi, Edie," she said, setting her latte on the podium. "Is Jacqueline here?" She pushed her sunglasses up over her glossy hair and glanced over at Mary and me. "Hi, Mary," she said, lips curling up into a devilish grin. "Welcome back."

She said nothing to me. I hated the way she called Chef Jackie *Jacqueline*, rhyming it with Vaseline. No, let me rephrase that. I hated *Sylvia*, period.

"Hi, Sylvia," Mary said. "Thanks." She pointed to Sylvia's latte. "That smells good. Is that a Lavazza roast?"

"No, it's Illy roast," Sylvia said. "From the Timberlake. You should try one."

"It does smell good," Mary said. "But I don't know about

that place. It's too expensive and it's always such a scene."
That was another thing about Mary. She had all the money in
the world but she didn't take it for granted. "Their lattes are
even more expensive than in New York." She turned to me.
"We'll go to Max's."

Sylvia, in her first acknowledgment of my presence, took
two steps toward me and said, "Don't you think the lattes at
the Timberlake are better?" Her eyes narrowed. "*Peggy*?"

She got my name right, which meant she was up to
something.

For a second, I hated myself for agreeing with Sylvia.
Timberlake's coffee *was* way better than Max's, and besides,
the guy at Max's always gave me a dirty look when I didn't
tip him. But then I realized what Sylvia was doing: She knew
Amber wouldn't be able to keep her mouth shut about Stephen
if Mary was at her counter ordering a latte.

I turned to Mary. "Max's is cheaper," I said.

"Well, it can't be any cheaper than *free*," Sylvia said.
Without looking down, she reached her hand into the purse
hanging from her elbow, and with two fingers, pulled out the
Timberline gift card she'd just purchased. She waved it at
Mary. "Merry Christmas, Mary," Sylvia said. She was smiling,
sort of. "A little late, sorry."

"Don't you mean a little *latte*?" said Edie. She didn't look up from her podium but her shoulders were giggle-shaking. "Cracking myself up," she mumbled.

Mary crinkled her forehead. "Thanks, Sylvia. Seriously, you shouldn't have."

No, I thought. She really shouldn't have. Mary reached out to take the card from Sylvia.

"Nice watch," Sylvia said. "Patek?"

"Mm-hmm. I'm sorry I didn't get anything for you," Mary said.

The weird thing is, I think she meant it. I mean, I wouldn't exactly say that she and Sylvia were friends, but after like four or five years of school together, they were sort of, I don't know, related. Like cousins who don't really know each other, or like each other, but still have to be nice at the barbecue.

Sylvia pointed at the gift card in Mary's hand and said, "Just make sure you get Amber to make yours," she said. "She makes the best lattes." Sylvia turned back to Edie. "Is Jacqueline here?"

"No," Edie said. "But she'll be back."

"Tell her to call me," Sylvia said. She felt for her sunglasses on top of her head. "Yes?"

"OK," Edie deadpanned. "Why?"

"Because I asked you to," Sylvia snapped back.

"I need more of a reason than that," Edie replied coolly. "Chef is very busy." Edie wasn't intimidated by Sylvia, and I admired that. No, I *envied* that.

Sylvia glared at Edie. "To discuss my schedule," she said firmly.

"Oh, no," Edie said. *"You're* working here?"

"Just tell her to call me. OK? Thanks." Sylvia smiled, a good fake one, and spun around to push through the velvet curtains and out the door. Her chignon caught a gust just outside the door, and it went horizontal for a second all in one piece, like a strap of leather. That's how hard the wind was blowing. And how hard her hair was. But her body didn't flinch, and her stilettos didn't wobble.

"Yikes," I muttered. Why would Sylvia work here? She was one of the wealthiest girls in Aspen. Her family moved here from L.A. when Sylvia's mother, a minor movie star from back in the early '90s, married some dot-com billionaire when Sylvia was ten.

Mary, she didn't need to work here either, but she did it because Jackie was some friend of a friend of her family, and besides she gave all her tips to the women's clinic down valley. Her family was so Kennedy that way.

But Sylvia? Something didn't add up. "What is she up to?" I said, knowing part of the answer already.

"Oh, she's harmless," Mary said. "She just tries to be dramatic." She waved her Timberline gift card at me. "Coffee?"

I really, really didn't want a coffee right now, especially from the Timberlake. But Mary grabbed my arm again and dragged me out the front door, like the perp on a cop show.

9

The walk over to the Timberlake was a quick one, especially that night. It was cold. A few snowflakes skipped through the air, but the sky was clear to the west, where the sun was skimming the top of the mountain. The yellow-orange light, not clear like daytime light but more like honey, reflected off the big dry flakes, turning them honey yellow-orange, too. It was like a sun shower, but with snow instead of rain. Maybe they call it a sunset-snow shower or something. I don't know. All I know is light like that doesn't happen very often.

But it happened on that night as we walked, and halfway to the Timberlake Mary stopped. "This," she said, raising her arms up to the sky, "is amazing." She squeezed my arm.

I wish I'd taken the chance to say to Mary, "Let's turn back. We can't go to the Timberlake. There's some gossip going down and it's about you. You're my best friend, and I want you to hear it from me, before it gets out of control." But I didn't.

Slow-roasted pork shoulder with jalapeño and cumin. Butterscotch sandwich cookies.

I squeezed back.

10

So far, today had sucked. But the worst thing that happened is what happened next.

The Timberlake was pretty much empty when we got there, except for two women sitting at a table smack in the middle of the room. They were both in zip-up shearling jackets, the blond one in deep brown, the dark-haired one in light tan. They each had shopping bags from Gucci, Tod's, and Pitkin County Dry Goods.

Amber was at the counter, with her back to us. She was listening intently to her cell phone, pressing it hard against one ear and pressing her finger over her other. "What?" she was yelling. "You're fading out!" She didn't even hear us come in.

Mary and I stood there for a moment. Amber didn't turn around. "I *know!*" she squawked. "I still can't believe it," she was saying. "Do you think it's true? Do you think she knows? I sure wouldn't want to tell her . . . What? You're fading out again!"

"Maybe we should go," I said. "How about Max's?"

Mary swatted me on the forearm playfully. "Let's make this gift card useful," she said.

"Yes, I can hear you!" Amber said, or more like shouted, into the phone. "Yes, that's what I heard! No, I would never tell anyone. I don't like to gossip." She paused for a moment. "I heard the girl is from Glenwood Springs or someplace down valley."

I grabbed Mary's arm. "Come on. Let's go to Max's. I'll buy." But this time, she didn't move.

"At his father's hotel!" Amber shouted. "Can you believe it? Janelle told me! She said that her brother's best friend delivered their room service the next morning. Yes, at the Durant!"

Mary's whole body stiffened. She brushed my hand off her arm.

"I *know.*" *Squawk.* "I can't believe it either. Stephen Haines. I *know!* A down valley girl! I wonder if Mary knows."

I walked around Mary and stood between her and

Amber. I looked up at Mary's face, which was rigid. Blank. Emotionless. I took both her arms and pushed, firmly backward. "Come on," I said. "Let's go to Max's."

"I *know!*" Amber squawked again.

That was the last squawk. It was Mary's turn to take the perp walk. I dragged her out of the shop. At the door, she said, "Let's go to Max's."

Amber never even turned around.

11

Back in Crawford Hall, after
Mary worked an entire dinner shift without cracking a joke
or even a smile, and after I spent four hours in the kitchen
biting my nails so far down that one of them started to bleed,
and after we'd brushed our teeth side by side in the shared
bathroom down the hall next to Veda St. Clair, who had the
biggest feet of any girl at MBSG, I tucked Mary into bed.

She was on the bottom bunk, and I wrapped her blanket
around her tightly, tucking it under the mattress to make it
snug like she was a little girl. She was wearing a zip-up hoodie
that said Broo/Klyn, with the hood pulled up and the strings
pulled so tight all you could see were her eyes and nose and
mouth.

I almost felt like I should lean down and kiss her on the cheek just to complete the ritual. It was something my mom did. No matter what else was going on, whether she was newly in love, or whether she was newly out of love, even when I wasn't speaking to her, she always tucked me in. And even if I ignored her when she did it, it made everything go away just long enough to put me to sleep. I guess she learned it from Granny.

I wanted to make everything go away for Mary.

But I didn't kiss her on the cheek. I just put a bottle of water on her nightstand and climbed up to my bunk.

I hated our bed. It was old and rickety, and every time one of us turned over the bed wiggled. The desks and chairs were the same way. It was weird—such an expensive school with such sucky rooms. But Mary had fixed ours up with a really plush saffron-colored rug and vibrant quilts and pillows. She painted the walls "Paparazzi," a soft peach white. She had blinds made for the windows, a soft green with a saffron thread running through them.

And of course there was Venus. I mean Aphrodite. Whoever.

Right now, with my reading light aimed haphazardly at Venus's feet, Venus looked slouchy. Her usually confident posture seemed to sag—heavy, tired.

I flipped off my reading light.

"It's just gossip," I said. "Really. Don't worry. Amber doesn't know what she's talking about." I didn't really believe that. I guess I said it because I wanted to make her feel better, but even I had to admit it was a pretty lame attempt. I was just trying to postpone the inevitable.

"Amber's never wrong," Mary said in the dark. It was the first time, ever, that I'd heard defeat in Mary's confident, optimistic voice. She sounded small, and it scared me.

"I wish I hadn't heard this from her."

I was laying on my back, but my heart still dropped to my stomach. I should have been the one to tell her.

Then she was quiet, but I knew she was crying, because the bed jerked with every silent sob. But I didn't say anything. I don't think she wanted me to. Instead, I just lay there, above her, and let her sobs rock me to sleep.

Poached pears with honey and whipped cream. Warm, chocolate-frosted brownies.

It didn't take long.

1

Classes didn't start for two more
days, so when I woke up at seven, I decided to take advantage
and go snowboarding. MBSG girls got free lift tickets on
weekdays, and besides, wasn't that part of the reason I came
here in the first place?

I'd been boarding five or six times already with Mary,
who'd taught me the basics. I wasn't an expert or anything,
but I could get up and down the mountain without sliding the
entire way down on my butt. I decided to let Mary sleep, and
let today be the first day I boarded on my own.

Besides, there'd be no drama on the mountain.

I was the first one in the dining hall, except for the
hairnetted Norma and Rosalind, who stood behind the steam

table sipping coffee and giggling. They were always laughing. I wondered what was really in their coffee cups.

I skipped the steam table and walked over to the cold-cereal bar. I mixed one spoonful of Life with one spoonful of Cap'n Crunch, then sprinkled Udi's Granola over both of them. After five months of cereal bar experience, I had dozens of cereal combinations, but this was the one I'd been craving.

I sat at the bench farthest from the entrance, with my back to the tall, mountain-facing windows behind me. The sky was blue, but the sun hadn't made it over the mountain yet. I loved this seat at breakfast because it was the first place the sun hit when it did manage its way over.

Girls started to trickle into the cafeteria. Pat, with her wild curls and rockabilly shoes, sat with her plate of breakfast sausages and cup of black coffee, reading an advanced algebra book. She must have known I was staring at her, because she looked up and nodded at me. I smiled and looked away. Nancy, with her pageboy haircut and cowl-neck sweater, was sharing a plate of scrambled eggs down table from me with Maggie, who had perfect vision but always wore vintage 1950s glasses. The Robinson sisters, plates loaded with home fries and slices of bacon, ate just beyond them. Lillian Bond, who cut her own bangs every morning, joined them. She didn't talk either.

I picked up my bowl and drank the last of the milk straight from it, which I knew would annoy my mother if she could see. Time to hit the mountain.

I took the chairlift all the way to the top of the mountain, checked the map for the longest, gentlest slope to the base, and took an hour to slide my way down. My form was wobbly, and I fell a few times, but twice I felt like I caught a nice groove, just making long, slow, lazy turns across the face of the trail and letting my body drive, instead of my brain.

It was sunny, brilliantly sunny. The only cloud in the periwinkle sky was trapped like a whipped cream topping on the tip of Castle Peak. Last night's snow was now a sprinkle of sparkly powder over the emerald trees. Blue, white, and green, like rugby stripes across the mountain. I inhaled deeply, the thin air coating and cooling the insides of my lungs.

If there was a more beautiful place in the world, I couldn't imagine it. I realized I was starting to stop noticing, lately, just how beautiful it was up here.

I tried to clear my mind and breathe. None of this was my business anyway, right? It wasn't my boyfriend sleeping with a shopgirl. It was Mary's. I'd learned, after three stepfathers and a mom who never wanted to listen or take my advice, when to mind my own business. I didn't have to worry about it. Right?

Wrong. Mary was my friend. My best friend. So that made it my business.

Even if I didn't want it to be.

On my second run down, I tried to just focus on the view, but it didn't work. I was too consumed with coming up with ways to get out of dealing with Mary's soon-to-be broken heart. Maybe if I wiped out, and broke my leg, I could go down to Denver for a few weeks and skip the ugly parts of what I knew was coming. I wouldn't have to be there when she cried, or come up with stupid things to say like "You don't need boys anyway." Or "He doesn't deserve you." Or "It's not you, it's him." Or "Let's have some ice cream. Ice cream is better than boys."

Or, "I know I should have told you right away so you didn't have to find out from Amber, but I just didn't know how. I'm still your best friend, right?"

Maybe that's what I was worried about the most. Because Mary had become my best friend. And I wasn't sure if I'd betrayed her or not.

That's when I wiped out. My board caught a corner of ice right underneath my feet and shot straight upward, sending me flying into the air and down onto my butt. The board came down onto the corner of my head, which, if I hadn't been wearing the dorky helmet I'd promised Mom I'd wear whenever I rode, would have probably knocked me into a coma.

But it wasn't a major wipeout, and I didn't break my leg. All I got was a bunch of snow down the back of my pants. So I took another run. This time, I tried coming up with scenarios in which Amber could be wrong. Maybe there's someone else who looks just like Stephen, who also stays at the Durant. Maybe Stephen has an evil twin. Maybe this shopgirl at Mod didn't even exist.

Maybe, somehow, Amber was wrong.

Like it or not, I was in it. Right smack in the middle of the drama. And I was going to find out the truth. I dropped off the mountain, stuck my board and snowpants in the shared locker area set aside at the base for MBSG, changed into jeans, and scarfed down a Lärabar.

I didn't have to be to work until later. Mod was just a few blocks from the base of the mountain. I decided to go try on some jeans.

2

I stomped my sneakers on the mat outside Mod's glass door. I realized I was wearing my old Pumas. Mary still had my new ones.

I pushed into the harshly lit store.

Every retailer in Aspen has a gimmick, and Mod's is this: It's supposed to look and feel like a laundry closet, all steel shelves and clotheslines with display jeans hanging from clothespins. It's a long and narrow store, over-outfitted with some kind of eco-friendly light that not only gave me a headache but turned everyone a strange SpongeBob color. Mirrors everywhere. Stacks and stacks of denim in every shade of, well, denim, from faded to overdyed to black to, yes, stonewashed. Skinny fit, loose fit, classic fit, low-rise-boot-cut-double-decaf-with-a-shot fit.

A sign on the front door claimed that Mod has "sizes for everyone." But they didn't mention that "everyone" only means size eight and under. Which kept me just barely in the game, but definitely limited my options.

Two girls about my age, salespeople or shopgirls or whatever you're supposed to call them (when I worked at Always 17 in Denver, we were called "associates"), were hunched over the checkout counter, whispering and comparing nail colors. Two look-alike thirty-something women with matching black-brown aviator jackets and mustard turtlenecks were tugging on the clothespinned display jeans and critiquing them in Spanish.

I was in my third year of Spanish but had no real idea what they were talking about, but judging from the six or seven pairs already hanging over the arms of the salesgirl who was following them around, I was guessing that it had something to do with how cheap these jeans were over here in America.

A mother and daughter stood in front of the three-way mirror to my left, craning their necks over their shoulders to compare asses. "Mine is so much bigger than yours," said the mother to the daughter. "I hate you."

Such *Lohans*, I thought, and for a moment I hated Aspen. Maybe I should have stayed on the mountain all day.

I grazed the shelves, stroking stacks of jeans and turning over the price tags in my fingers, pretending not to be shocked. 120 dollars. 166 dollars. 370 dollars. Out of effing control. The Levi's I had on cost me thirty-four bucks. Maybe that's why the salesgirls weren't drooling all over me like they were drooling all over those Spanish women. Or Argentine. Or Venezuelan. Or who knows. My Spanish wasn't good enough to know.

I wondered if one of the salesgirls was Crystal. I grabbed a pair of 139-dollar Earls and ambled over to the counter and waved them at girl #1. "Can I try these on?" I scanned their chests for nametags, but I guess salesgirls don't wear nametags in Aspen.

"Are those the cheap Earls?" said salesgirl #1, sighing. "Size eight?" She looked at my hips. She held out her hand to salesgirl #2. "Brett, hand me those keys." So #2 was not Crystal.

The counter phone rang as salesgirl #1 led me toward the back of the store. "Mod," said salesgirl #2. Then, after a pause, "Jules! Line one!" Salesgirl #3, the one following around the Spanish speakers, yelled, "Thanks." Not Crystal.

Salesgirl #1 led me to a bank of four curtains suspended

from a wire frame bolted to the ceiling. They weren't exactly dressing "rooms"; they were more like booths, only instead of walls they were separated by curtains. Each one had a standing mirror, small clothes rack, and a steel folding chair. Very Mod.

"Thanks," I said, just as Brett yelled over from the counter. "Dennie! I'm going to get lattes. Want one?" Not Crystal. Strike three. Maybe Amber *was* wrong, because there didn't seem to be a Crystal at Mod.

I slid into the farthest booth on the left and drew the curtain shut. Which, weirdly, plunged me into near total darkness. There was no light in the booth, only whatever snuck in underneath the curtains. I could barely see the jeans I'd brought in there. I felt for my folding chair and sat down. I slipped off my jeans and sat there in my boy-briefs.

Just then, I heard a voice, a girl's voice, one I didn't recognize, coming through the curtain from the booth next to mine. Low, deep, purring quietly.

"No, you shouldn't break your date with her. I just really wanted to see you, that's all."

Even though there was no one there to see, I rolled my eyes. Yet another lonely cheating heart in Aspen. What a shocker. Stop the presses. I felt for the Earls and started to snake my feet through the legs.

"Don't worry about it," purred the voice. "I mean, I knew about her before all of this ever started."

I pulled the Earls up over my hips. If these were an eight, I needed a ten.

The voice morphed from a purr to a whimper. "It's OK. I understand. It's OK, Stephen."

Stephen? I froze, zipper half-up. Oh, my God. Could this be Crystal? Suddenly, I wished I hadn't come to Mod at all.

"I know," she whimpered. "I've just been bummed out all day, that's all." Pause. "Oh, nothing important. I just got a really mean e-mail from my father. He wants me to move out."

I didn't move. Then I realized it would be conspicuous not to move so I shimmied to one side and rustled my curtain. I started to pull down my jeans.

"Nothing really. He's always said I'd have to leave when I turned eighteen and, well, today's my birthday. Yeah, I know. Eighteen. The big one." Pause.

Really, I thought. Her birthday? Hmm. It seemed too perfect. She seemed like she was working a little hard. I was stuck between shock and suspicion, between wanting to know nothing and needing to know more, and I didn't even have my pants all the way on.

"No, no plans to celebrate or anything. But that's OK. I can just watch television or something."

"Or maybe I can go visit my grandfather in the hospice."
Pause. "Yeah, he moved there a few days ago. They say he's
only got a few weeks left."

This was over the top, I thought. If that was Mary's
Stephen, and he was falling for this, he was more stupid than
I ever thought he was. Or else he was totally whipped.

"Really, Stephen? No, no. I couldn't ask you to . . ." Pause.
"Well, if you don't think Mary would mind."

Mary. Holy effing cow. This really was Crystal. And she
was talking to Stephen Haines.

Overload. I started cooking.

*Grilled pizza with mozzarella cheese and fresh basil. Pork
roast with rosemary potatoes.*

Maybe it wasn't Crystal. Stephen and Mary were really
common names, after all. I still didn't know for sure.

Pound cake with lemon curd and whipped cream.

"It would be really hot to see you." Pause. Her voice was
throaty now, older. "Maybe we should get a room at your hotel
again." Pause, and a giggle. "I know it's not exactly *your* hotel.
But it is, kind of, right? I mean, one day it will be."

What an operator. She must be amazing looking for
Stephen, or anyone, to be buying this. Or else she had
something really special to offer. I didn't have to wonder too
hard what it could be.

The voice was lilting now, happy. "I can't believe you almost stood me up for your girlfriend. Silly." Pause. "Oh, I'm just kidding. I'll see you later. I gotta get back to work." Pause. "Bye, sexy."

I sat back down and took the Earls all the way off. If this was Crystal, which I wasn't sure it was, not yet, not really, but if it was her, she was dishing it out. And the Prince of Aspen, if that's who she was talking to, and I still wasn't a hundred percent sure about that either, not really, not yet, well, he was buying it.

I pulled open my curtain, just a crack, just enough to eyeball this girl as she stepped back into the store. Which she did a moment later.

She was, like the other salesgirls, totally covered in denim. Low-rise faded jeans with a slight flare over her distressed motorcycle boots. Shiny black denim vest on top of a tight, just a little too short white tank. No belt. Woven leather cuff on her left hand. Wavy, dark brown hair in a rockstar cut. Tan, but not from the tanning salon, more like naturally tan. Golden. Hazy eyes. Undeniably beautiful. Tough-looking, but beautiful. I couldn't believe she was interested in dating a guy who was still in high school, no matter how rich he was.

Suddenly, the curtain that was two booths over swept

open. Sylvia strode out in a pair of the most expensive jeans in the shop, a limited edition from some French designer whose name I wouldn't be able to pronounce even if someone French took the time to teach me how.

Oh, my God. Sylvia! She must have heard the whole conversation, too. I closed my curtain a little farther, just barely peeking through.

Sylvia crossed over to the mirror on the wall opposite the booths. She turned around to get a look at her butt, and for a second, a tiny, split second, she looked over at the crack in my curtain. Her jungle-red lips curled up at the corners, and her left eyebrow cocked straight up. It was a smile I'd never seen before, one Granny never mentioned.

She turned back around. "Excuse me," she barked, staring at herself in the mirror. "Hey, you." She snapped her fingers at Crystal. "These are too big."

Crystal turned slowly, spinning her body first, then flipping her head around with a jerk, tossing her hair out of her face. "I'm sorry, do you need something?" Her smile was gritty and tight.

"Yes." Sylvia's eyes ricocheted off the mirror and directly into Crystal's. She ran her thumb under the waistband of her jeans and pulled them forward off her hips. "I could swim in these. I need a size two." She looked back into her own eyes and raised her hand to smooth her hair, stopping just short of actually touching it. It was already perfect, of course.

Crystal walked up behind Sylvia. "Oh?" She dropped her eyes to Sylvia's butt, which she slowly and methodically took in from a few different angles. She tugged Sylvia's waistband upward with a jerk, throwing Sylvia off balance. "Are you, um, sure? These seem pretty snug to me."

Sylvia slapped Crystal's hands away from her waistband. "Don't touch me," she hissed. "Size two."

I pulled my curtain shut and changed back into my thirty-four-dollar jeans.

3

𝓘 spent the next two hours sitting
on a bench in Wagner Park, hiding behind my sunglasses.
Oh, and freaking the eff out.

I got the same text from Mary, twice:

where r u

But I didn't answer.

Why couldn't I have broken my leg on the slopes?

I hated myself for thinking it, but I did. I couldn't help
wishing the gossip wasn't true, wishing I didn't care, wishing
I wasn't here. But I did care. I cared because I loved Mary.
And I was here.

I didn't want her to go through this. I wanted to protect her. I didn't want to be the one to ruin her life. I knew I had to tell her, I knew that's what friends did, but for two hours all I could do was sit in the cold wishing I'd broken my leg and searching everywhere I could think of for some guts.

But I couldn't find any.

4

"It's just gossip, Mary," Chef Jackie was saying. I still had my sunglasses on, but I could see through the pass-through that Chef Jackie was wearing her FDNY bandanna. I could also hear her. "This is Aspen. People have way too much time on their hands. Gossip is the town sport. If you ignore it long enough, it will pass. It always does."

I couldn't see Mary but I heard her. "I know. You're right. It's just gossip. It's just," she groaned, loudly. "I know they say it doesn't matter if you have a boyfriend or not. But, I like having a boyfriend. I think Stephen and I . . ."

I pushed my way through the swinging door and into the kitchen, cutting her off. "Hi."

"Hi," Mary said. She was still in the same Broo/Klyn hoodie she slept in, sitting on a metal folding chair wedged in beside the dishwashing sink, sliding slowly forward off the chair then catching herself with her Pumas, I mean my Pumas, which she was still wearing. "Where have you been?"

"I was on the mountain," I said, truthfully. "Are you OK?"

Mary nodded. "I tried to call you," she said.

"I must have been out of range," I said. "Sorry." I looked down at my second-string sneakers.

"She's fine," Chef Jackie said. "It's just gossip. Trust me, you'll know the truth when you see him next. Guys can't lie. Just check the eyes." She was standing in front of the gleaming black-and-stainless steel Berkel, which she'd set on the counter under the pass-through. It was as big as a curled-up Labrador, only about a hundred times heavier. Jackie was swiping a head-size block of prosciutto back and forth across the whirring blade, catching the translucent slices on a piece of parchment paper. "And in the meantime, relax. He's a good guy, right?"

"Um," I said.

"What?" Chef Jackie said. She pointed at a foot-long, bloodred hard sausage at the far end of the counter. "Peggy, hand me that salami."

Mary blew up into her bangs, sending them flying across her face. "He is a good guy." She blew again. "He's better than a good guy. He's the best guy." Then her voice got really little. "He's *my* guy."

I picked up the salami, which took two hands because it was way heavier than it looked, and handed it to Jackie. "Mary?" I said.

"Yeah?"

"Um," I said again.

"I say give him the benefit of the doubt," Jackie said, saving me from my inability to form a sentence. She used a tiny paring knife to slice the tip off one end of the salami. She hoisted it and aimed it at the Berkel's whirring blade. "And if he screwed up," she said, pressing the salami into the blade, which deepened the whir, "dump him." Slices of salami started flying everywhere. "Damn, I love this thing," said Jackie.

Mary sniffled. Jackie cackled.

Was it just me or was it funny that Jackie was slicing a salami right at that moment?

Chef Jackie sliced all the way through the foot-longer, then switched off the Berkel. "I have to get this thing out from under the pass-through," she said. She reached over to unplug it. "Peggy, help me move this over by the freezer."

I did, and it wasn't easy. It weighed about a million pounds. But we managed to wedge it between the freezer and one of the prep sinks. "Not a very high-profile location," Chef Jackie said. "This thing needs a VIP corner." She sighed. "We need a bigger kitchen."

"You know what sucks the most?" Mary said. "I haven't even talked to him yet. All we've done is text message."

Is that really what sucks the most? I thought. It seemed to me thinking your boyfriend was screwing some girl would be the part that sucks the most.

"What time are you meeting him at Matsuhisa?" Chef Jackie said.

"Eight thirty."

"You'll know the truth by eight thirty-five," Jackie said. "Check the eyes."

5

At exactly 8:19, Mary burst into
the busy Reno kitchen, knocking a grilled porterhouse and
side of broccoli rabe off the warming counter and onto the
floor with a colossal crash. Jackie, bent over a sauce on
the stove, shot me a look. I dove for a broom and started
sweeping. I pushed Mary toward the back of the room as I
swept.

Four-cheese potatoes au gratin. Seared tuna with miso glaze.

I'd cleaned the whole mess up, including all the shards
of plate, before noticing that Mary, who'd collapsed into the
same folding chair she'd been draped over this afternoon,
was holding her open cell phone out for me. Her quilted
jacket was unzipped, and her forehead was all scrunched up.

She stared at it for a moment. She chewed on her lip. Then she looked at me again and handed me the phone, still open.

On the screen was a text from Stephen, sent at 8:07.

> can't make matsu.
> will explain. s

"That could mean anything, Mary. He could have a flat tire. His mother could be sick. You don't know for sure. Right, Chef?" But Chef Jackie didn't hear. She was focused on her sauce.

"Peggy," Mary said. Her scrunched-up forehead started to quiver.

I closed the phone and tucked it into Mary's jacket pocket. She stood up and leaned forward, into me. I held her.

Linguine with sautéed gremolata shrimp. Warm strawberry pie with butterscotch ice cream. Crispy falafel with mint yogurt sauce.

"It's OK, Mary," I lied. "It will be OK."

1

"Order up!"

As usual, during service, Chef Jackie was all business. Her eyes went crystal clear and her chin went down. She leaned into whatever she was cooking, hovering over her food like a kindergartner over a coloring book.

"Order!" Chef Jackie yelled again. She didn't like repeating herself, especially during dinner service. "I can't afford to lose focus during service," she told me once. "If you get behind even by a single order, the rest of the evening is shot."

Reno had been impossibly busy tonight, packed solid. So far Chef Jackie, Emma, and Graciela had sent nine duck confit salads, seven pork loin entrées, twelve chicken specials, and seventeen mixed salumi plates into the dining room. It proved the Berkel was a hit.

Jackie was crouched over a flatiron steak. She looked up at the pass-through, which was crowded with salads. "Order up!" she shouted. "Whose salads are those?"

"Sylvia's" I said.

"I'm shocked," Chef Jackie said.

I couldn't believe Sylvia was actually working here. I never would have imagined it. I wondered what she was up to. It must be something major, because she would never lower herself to actually working. She might break a nail, or lose an eyelash, or whatever happens to wax-figure girls like Sylvia.

But it was her first night on the floor, and judging from her performance so far, her first night ever working at all. Her beet salads, due out to table four about five minutes ago, were starting to wilt and bleed in the heat of the kitchen, while Sylvia was just, well, missing.

Missing isn't the right word. We all knew where she was. She was in the ladies' room, spit-sculpting her hair and re-applying that jungle lipstick. I wondered if she would wash her hands before returning to the floor, like the sign in there says employees are supposed to.

"*Where the hell is Sylvia?*" Chef Jackie shouted.

"Want me to get her?" I said.

"No, I want you to take those salads out," she said.

"But my jacket," I said, pointing to my chef's jacket, which was stained with beet juice and made me look like a serial killer chef. Jackie insisted on clean shirts in the dining room; she even kept a spare chef's jacket for herself for when she'd circulate in the dining room greeting customers.

"I don't care," she said. "Get out there." She spun around to Emma, who'd slipped one foot out of its black Croc to scratch her other leg with her toe. A drizzle of burgundy sauce ran down her otherwise immaculate chef's jacket and checked pants. "Did you fire that halibut yet?" barked Jackie.

"On it," said Emma.

"Peggy, wait," Chef Jackie said. "Taste this." She handed me a tasting spoon with a dot of burgundy sauce on its tip. I wiped it on my tongue and smacked my lips.

"It's OK," I said.

"Tell the truth," Jackie said.

"Too flat," I said. "Sweet. It needs acid."

"OK, go," Chef Jackie said, reaching for a bottle of Banyuls vinegar.

I smoothed my jacket and grabbed the three plates from the kitchen side of the pass-through. I balanced them precariously on my forearms and pushed my way, backward, through the swinging door and into the dining room.

It was all but full, with every table occupied and only a couple of them with empty seats. Edie was holding court up front, juggling two waiting parties and a phone call. Charlie Parker was playing on the stereo, just loud enough to hear it above the din of chatter and glass-clinking, but not enough to identify it. I knew it was Charlie Parker because that's all Chef Jackie ever played here.

I wove my way past a fat guy bound for the bathroom, two skinny Russian women who appeared to be going table to table and chatting with customers, and Mary, who had that look on her face, that pale look with black circles and glazed eyes, that no-sleep look that you couldn't fake. I couldn't believe she was working, but I couldn't imagine what else she'd do, either.

"Where do these go?" I mouthed.

"Sylvia's?" she mouthed back. I nodded. "Four," she said.

I looked at her blankly. I had no clue where four was. Mary pointed at a table of four women, all of whom were staring at me, intensely. "Thank you," I whispered to Mary. I groaned and made my way over to them.

"Your salads," I chirped pleasantly. I slid the three dishes onto table four.

"It's about time," said the blondest one.

"Where is my appetizer?" demanded the one with the fakest red hair I'd ever seen. "I ordered the soup."

"Of course," I smiled. "I'll be right back with your soup."

"Where is our waitress?" the one with the most rings asked.

"She'll be right back," I answered. I had no idea whether it was true, but it seemed like the right thing to say.

"I doubt that," she said to her friends, who scoffed in unison. Then she pointed at my jacket. "Are you the chef?"

"No," I said, stifling a scowl. "I just work here."

"Well, tell the chef we want to speak to him," she said. "About the service."

"I'll let *her* know," I said. "Be right back with your soup." It was hard to smile on cue, especially at a really annoying customer who thinks that Sylvia is my fault, but I pulled off a grin nonetheless. A real-looking one. Granny would have been proud.

I sucked in my gut and wormed my way past a woman waiting outside the ladies' room door. "Excuse me," she said. She reattached her clip-on earring, which was probably worth more than my mother's house. "Is there another ladies' room?"

"I'm sorry," I said, without stopping. "Just this one." I

straight-armed my way into the kitchen. "Soup!" I shouted. "Table four." I grabbed a bowl, ducked under Emma, stepped over Graciela's feet, and ladled the soup into the bowl. "This soup needs fire," I said. I turned up the flame.

I bolted back out the swinging door, wiping a dribble from the side of the bowl with my kitchen towel. I noticed the line for the ladies' room was now three deep. I delivered the soup to table four without a word, then marched over to Edie.

"Is she still in there?" I asked, teeth gritted.

"What do you think?" Edie answered. The phone rang. "Edie, this is Reno. I mean, Reno, this is Edie."

I walked forcefully over to the ladies' room line. "Excuse me," I chirped. I knocked on the locked door. "Are you OK?"

There was no answer. I turned to face the line of women. "I'm sure she's fine," I said, trying to smile. "I, uh, it'll be just a minute."

Just then, Mary appeared. She touched the first woman on the shoulder. "Follow me." She knocked on the men's room door, then unlatched it. Empty. "Hope you don't mind," she said, smiling.

"Thank you," said the woman. "Thank you."

I looked at Mary. "Thanks," I mouthed. "You OK?"

"Fine," Mary said out loud. Then, abruptly, "Really."

"OK," I said, not believing her but having no other choice than to take her word for it. "Grilled cheese sandwiches. Tonight. Venus. Be there."

Sylvia pushed into the kitchen about five minutes later, eyes red but hair perfect. She slipped her phone into her apron. "Where's my order?" She looked at me. "Penny? Where are my salads?"

Eff off, I thought. My name is Peggy.

Butterflied chicken breast with bacon and oven-dried tomatoes. Citrus risotto. Cherry clafouti.

"You missed it," snarled Jackie. "Don't do that again." She looked up from the stove. "Ever." She walked over and took Sylvia by the shoulder. "And her name," she said, staring into Sylvia's eyes but pointing at me with her tongs, "is Peggy. Not Penny. You got that?"

Sylvia inhaled deeply. "Fine," she said.

2

It was after midnight when Mary and I walked home from work. It was freezing, probably ten degrees at the most, so I had all the heavy gear on: parka, ski hat, gloves, scarf. But there was a full moon reflecting off the snow, and it was beautiful, so I didn't mind that Mary was walking so slow.

People always say that when the moon is full in the winter, it's just like daytime, because its reflection on the snow makes everything so bright white. But they're wrong. It's nothing like daytime. When it's a full moon in the mountains, everything, especially the snow, is blue.

We dodged a few drunk tourists, probably stumbling home from an evening of vodka shots at the Sky Hotel. "Partee!" one of them yelled into the silent blue.

"What a loser," I said. "Can you believe what a disaster Sylvia was tonight?"

"That poor girl," Mary said. Then she snickered. Just a little. But I heard it.

We turned left and headed up the hill to Crawford Hall, which loomed in the blueness over Garmisch Street like a chaperone. It, too, was blue, a serious blue, square and asleep except for the lights that lined its walkway.

I pulled my ski cap down over my head. "Have you heard from Stephen today?" I asked.

"No," she said. "I haven't." And that's all she said.

I guess she didn't want to talk about it. So I just walked next to her, as slowly as she wanted to, looking at the blue snow under my feet, cooking apple crumble in my head, and wondering why anyone would bother to fall in love.

3

So later that night, really late, like
way after one when I was making grilled cheese sandwiches
on the George Foreman Grill next to the stack of books on my
desk, and Mary was sitting on the saffron carpet, leaning up
against Venus with her eyes closed, there was a knock at the
door.

"Is something burning?" came the voice.

Sylvia.

Mary looked at me blankly, then got up and went over
to the door. "No," she said, opening the door. "Peggy's
cooking."

Sylvia was standing in the doorway, wearing a black zip-
up hoodie over black leggings and black ballet slippers. She

seemed so much shorter, so much smaller, when she wasn't in stilettos.

"Oh," she said. She backed slowly out of the doorway and started walking down the hall.

Mary glanced over at me quizzically, then stepped out into the hallway after Sylvia. "Are you hungry?" she called out.

Ugh, I thought. I can't believe she's inviting her in here. But that was Mary. Always nice. Right then, it annoyed me. Funny how that happens.

"Me?" Sylvia said from the hallway. I couldn't see her, but she sounded honestly surprised. I'd never heard that in her voice before. She always seemed like she knew everything already. I didn't think there actually *were* such things as surprises in Sylvia's life.

"Yes, you," Mary said. "Did you eat tonight?"

"I, uh, I don't, I . . ." Sylvia's words stumbled, uncharacteristically unconfidently, out of her mouth. She probably hadn't. Come to think of it, I'd certainly never seen her consume anything other than lattes and Diet Cokes.

I looked up to see Mary leading Sylvia in by the arm. "Peggy always puts butter on both sides of the bread," Mary said. She threw a couple pillows onto the floor next to Venus. "And she uses two kinds of cheese and a little bit of mustard on the inside. They taste better that way. Don't they, Peggy?" Mary sat down on a pillow and smiled up at me. Sylvia sat down next to her.

I scraped a sandwich onto a paper plate, then cut it in half to let the cheese (cheddar and Gouda, for the record, the best grilled-cheese combo ever, until I find another one) ooze out a little. I handed it to Sylvia.

"Thanks," she said. She turned and looked me directly in the eye, for only a split second. "Peggy."

At least she got my name right. She was no dummy.

I handed the other sandwich to Mary and started two more. One for me and one for luck.

That was something my grandmother taught me. *Margaret*, she'd say. *You never know. Always make enough for unexpected visitors. It's good luck. I always did that, and look how lucky I've been.* Then, she'd cup my face in her hands and kiss me on the nose. *I have you.*

Mary and Sylvia ate their sandwiches in silence. Besides the hiss of the George Foreman, the only sounds in the room were the faint crunch of toasted bread and the rustle of a paper napkin.

Grilled sourdough bread with garlic butter. Smashed new potatoes with Asiago cheese.

By the time I'd finished grilling the second round of

sandwiches, Sylvia had cleaned her plate. I was amazed. The girl really is capable of eating.

I handed Sylvia another half-sandwich from the extra I'd made. She took one bite, then set it down. I saw something splatter next to it. It made a wet spot on the plate.

I looked up, and could see the trail the tear had taken down her cheek and off the tip of her chin. She sniffed. It was something I'd never imagined.

Mary put her sandwich down and laid her hand on Sylvia's knee. "It's OK. It's hard, I know. Waiting tables is the hardest job in the world."

Sylvia closed her eyes.

"OK," Mary said. "Maybe running the UN is harder." She ducked her head down underneath Sylvia's face, looking up at her and smiling hopefully.

Sylvia didn't smile back. She just inhaled sharply. I thought for a moment she was going to cry for real. You know, sobs and sniffles and all. But she didn't. Maybe this *was* real crying, for Sylvia.

Mary reached over and grabbed Sylvia's forearm. "You don't have to work, Sylvia. You can quit," she said. "Tomorrow. Just tell Jackie you quit. Problem solved."

I put the last sandwich on the last plate and sat down on the floor next to Mary.

"No," Sylvia said. "I can't." Her voice was shaking.

"Sylvia, be serious," Mary said. "Neither one of us needs this job."

"I do," Sylvia said. "My stepfather is taking away my allowance."

"Why?" Mary asked.

"It's his power trip over my mother," Sylvia said. She wasn't even close to crying now, just cold.

I searched for a reason to feel sorry for Sylvia. I tried to imagine what it must be like for her, to have an unlimited allowance suddenly cut off. I tried to put myself in her shoes.

But somehow, I just couldn't jam my feet into those patent-leather stilettos.

"Whatever," Sylvia said. "You've got your own problems." She took another bite of sandwich. "I heard about, you know." She looked over at Mary.

Mary just stared back.

"You're not the only one," Sylvia said.

"What do you mean?" Mary yanked her hand off Sylvia's forearm and crossed her arms. "The only one what?"

"The only one whose boyfriend sleeps around."

"You have a boyfriend?" I blurted out. This was news to me. Sylvia just didn't seem the type to lower herself to actually having a boyfriend.

"In Denver," she said. "At culinary school." She stood up and walked over to Mary's desk and took a Kleenex. She blew her nose. "Howie. I don't know for sure if he's cheating, of course."

It was hard enough to believe she had a boyfriend, but it was another thing entirely that his name was *Howie*. It seemed like Sylvia would date a Preston or a Spencer or a Giovanni. Not a Howie.

"I don't know for sure, either," Mary said. "Except that I do." She looked up at Sylvia and locked eyes with her. They stared each other down, half threatening each other, half downloading from each other, for too long. I had to pipe up to try and break the stare.

"Maybe Stephen has a good explanation!" I said. "Maybe it's not another girl. "

But Mary's eyes didn't flinch, and neither did Sylvia's. "Give me a break. It's always another girl," Sylvia said.

"Is it?" Mary said.

"Always." Sylvia finally looked away. "What else could it be?"

"Uh," I interrupted, clumsily. "About a billion trillion other things. He could have a twin, for instance." It was the first thing I thought of and really stupid.

Sylvia and Mary looked at me, then at each other. Then

they both burst out laughing, simultaneously, a manic, aggressive laugh.

"You know what I mean," I stuttered over their weird laughter. "You know what I mean."

Cedar-plank salmon with bitter greens and pine nuts. Barbecued chicken wings with Vietnamese spices.

Mary patted my arm. "It's OK, Peggy," she said, still chuckling, which made me feel even more stupid.

I dropped my last bite of grilled cheese onto my plate and stood up to put away the bread and cheese and mustard and butter. "You're right," she said, taking a deep breath. "He could have a twin."

"What are you going to do?" Sylvia said.

"I don't know," Mary said. Then, her voice went really low. "But I kind of want to see her."

"Who?" I asked.

"Her," Mary repeated. Her face was stern and red and wide-awake. This no-sleep girl suddenly had all the energy in the world.

1

Mary got up way early on Wednesday.
She spent twenty minutes in the shower, which was fifteen minutes more than normal. She blew her hair dry, which I'd never seen before; in fact, I never even knew she had a blow-dryer. She tried on three different outfits, which was three more than usual, before settling on a pair of slim gray herringbone trousers and a camel cashmere tank-cardigan sweater set. She pulled her hair back into a chignon, which she secured with a silver clasp. She applied, then reapplied, mascara. She fastened a simple gold chain around her neck and two tiny gold hoops into her ears. After she pulled on her shiniest equestrian riding boots and zipped them up, she said "There."

She looked beautiful, I guess. But different. Something was missing from her eyes.

All this took her ninety minutes, which was eighty-five minutes more than I spent on my entire cargo pant and wool pullover ensemble.

Mary didn't say a word at breakfast, where she ate half an English muffin with butter and grape jelly, and I ate a Rice Krispies–Frosted Flakes combo. She just smiled and nodded at Fiona and Angie, who came over to compliment her sweater set, pointing at her mouth, which was full of English muffin. Saryn, wandering through the dining hall looking for a seat, accidentally bumped Mary in the head with the corner of her tray but Mary just smiled and waved her on.

Moroccan couscous with crispy chickpeas.

She stayed clammed up right through Western Civ, just shrugging and shaking her head when Ms. Murfin asked her how her winter break was.

Wok-fried prawns with ginger and bok choy.

Even in Biology lab, where we really didn't have to do anything except sign out the equipment we'd be using this semester and go over the syllabus, Mary wouldn't chat.

Old-fashioned apple cake with cinnamon veins.

In fact, the first thing she said to me all day was at lunch, when we were sitting across from each other in the middle of the cafeteria, poking at the same plate of steamed sesame broccoli from the salad bar. "What was her name again?"

I pretended I didn't hear. "I'm getting some fries," I said. "I'll be right back."

I came back with fries and an egg salad sandwich to share, but Mary didn't touch it so I ate her half for her.

"Crystal?" she said.

I pretended again that I didn't hear.

2

I didn't know it was coming, not
exactly, but I wasn't really all that surprised when after classes
got out, Sylvia was waiting in front of Crawford Hall for Mary
and me. Well, she was really waiting for Mary, I guess. But I
was there, too.

Sylvia was wearing a fitted black parka, which fell to
midthigh. Belted. Her black stiletto boots were zipped up
over her blue-black jeans. Her hair, of course, was flawless.

I wondered, now that she and Mary had bonded over my
grilled cheese sandwiches, did it mean that Sylvia was going
to be hanging around all the time? I hoped not. I preferred
Sylvia to be a topic of thirdhand speculation, not someone I
had to deal with at close range.

"Let's go shopping," she said as we approached. She grabbed Mary's hand. "Come on."

Sylvia started dragging her down the hill. Mary looked back at me. This was the last thing I wanted to do. But I knew I couldn't say no, because if I said no, then Mary would have insisted, and I would have protested, and she would have double insisted, and it would have been this whole big thing, and besides, I didn't want to let her out of my sight because she was freaking me out, which I realized was so different than yesterday, when I was kind of trying to avoid her. Could things have changed that much?

It took me about three steps before I realized where Sylvia was headed.

Mod.

Garlic-roasted buffalo tenderloin.

3

"*That one?*" Mary said, squaring her shoulders and pointing across the racks of jeans at Crystal, who'd just pushed through the Employees Only door back by the changing booths. She was decked, surprise surprise, in denim: jeans, a tight-fitting denim jacket, and a ribbed tank, black this time. The same motorcycle boots she wore on Monday. Three rings on three different fingers. I hated to admit it, but she was hot.

Crystal walked straight over to the checkout counter without looking up to see who was in the store. Unlike Mary and Sylvia, who had been camped out at the fitting booths waiting for her. Mary had already tried on three pairs of jeans. They all looked great on her, but she wasn't going to buy them. I knew that.

"Yes," said Sylvia. "That one." She reached into her purse and pulled out her lipstick. "Here. Jungle red."

Mary paused a moment, looked over at Sylvia, and took the lipstick. She dabbed a little on her lower lip, then a little on her upper lip, then she mushed her lips together. It was shocking to see her with that kind of lipstick. She looked like a different person, glamorous but dangerous. It was still Mary, but her eyes had changed.

"Are you sure?" Mary said. "That one?" She pointed again at Crystal.

"I'm sure," Sylvia said.

Mary's squared shoulders bowed, and for a moment, she looked like herself again. "Oh, I don't know." She ducked into her booth.

I pretended not to see any of it. For the second time this week, I was faking like I was shopping at Mod. Only this time, I was here for her. For Mary. I was worried about her. And even if part of me still didn't want to be here, I *was* here, and I was staying.

Penne pasta with pulled pork and olives. Thick-cut potato chips with coarse sea salt and vinegar.

"Excuse me!" Sylvia snapped at Crystal, who was

folding jeans on a display next to the fitting booths. "Excuse me."

Crystal sighed, and without turning around said, "Yes?"

"Over here," Sylvia said. "My friend here in the fitting room, if you can call it that, needs a different size. My friend *Mary*. She's over here."

Crystal turned around slowly. She recognized Sylvia from the other day. I figured she could smell a setup. But she was trapped. And besides, she couldn't resist the bait. Sylvia knew this; in fact, she counted on it.

"Oh?" Crystal smiled. "Your friend Mary? And what does *Mary* need?"

Sylvia narrowed her eyes at Crystal.

Suddenly, with a *whoosh*, Mary pulled back the curtain, standing there in nothing but a white tank and bikini bottoms. She looked incredible, muscular and confident. "You're Crystal, aren't you?" she said, drawing out the word "aren't" into several syllables. I held my breath. Mary held out her hand. "I'm Mary. Mary Moorhead. Perhaps Stephen has told you about me."

Crystal drew in a sharp breath, clearly shocked. "Hello," she choked. But she recovered quickly, flipping her hair and steadying her gaze. "Do you need a size?"

Mary looked Crystal up and down, pausing at her crotch.

"No, I don't think I need any help after all. There's *nothing* here."

Crystal said coolly, "I guess you'll just have to go someplace else."

Crystal turned back to the jeans display and started folding.

Mary gathered up the heap of jeans she'd tried on and thrust it at Crystal. "Here." Crystal didn't turn around, so Mary dropped them onto the floor at her feet. She looked over at Sylvia. "I'm not worried about *her*," she said. "Stephen has *taste*." She closed her curtain.

Crystal knelt down, picked up the pile of jeans, and quickly walked away.

I just stood there, unsure what to think. I'd given up the jeans-browsing front. I was, I believe *agog* is the word. What had just happened and where was my *nice* Mary?

Beef skewers with grilled broccoli and black bean sauce. Whole trout stuffed with sage and bacon. Creamed spinach.

"Your mouth is hanging open," Sylvia said.

I effing hated her, but she was right. My mouth was hanging open. I closed it with a clack.

4

𝓘 was sitting on the floor in front
of Venus, pretending that I was flipping through *Snowboarder*
magazine, but really just biting my nails and cooking in my
head and freaking out.

Braised squab with apple cider and maple reduction.

Mary was in the shower.

Her cell phone rang. It was on her bunk, and I really
didn't want to look, but I couldn't help seeing the caller ID
display. Well, maybe I could have helped it if I hadn't crawled
across the saffron floor and picked up her phone and looked
at it, but I couldn't help it.

It said: Stephen

"No surprise there," I said to Venus, tossing the phone back on her bunk.

She didn't answer.

"Your butt rang," I said, when she came back into the room with a chocolate brown towel wrapped around her head and a beige bath sheet wrapped around her body.

She picked up her phone and looked at the display. Then put it back down.

Mary positioned herself in front of the mirror, unwrapped her head and picked up a comb. Drawing it through, she slicked her hair off her face and secured it straight back with a headband. She squeezed a dollop of moisturizer into her hands and, leaning into the mirror, carefully massaged it upward into her forehead, then her cheekbones, then across her chin, curling her lip under and stretching out her neck. She Q-tipped one ear, and then the other, muttering "Gross" as she tossed the Q-tip into the wastebasket. She rifled for a second through her makeup bag, then pulled out a mascara wand. She unscrewed it, then, making a strained O shape with her mouth, swept it across her eyelashes. She dropped her towel and stepped into a pair of boy-briefs. She pumped a handful of yellow lotion into her palms and rubbed them together before smoothing the lotion onto her left calf.

Just then her phone rang again. "Can you get that?" she said, waving her lotiony hands at me. "I'm greasy."

I crawled back across the saffron to her bunk, making it there by the third ring. "It's Sylvia," I said, reading the display.

"Get it!" shouted Mary.

I didn't want to talk to Sylvia. At all. So I pretended to fumble with the phone, like I had no idea how to flip it open and answer a call. It rang again, and again. "What kind of phone is this?" I asked. "How do you get it open? Help!"

Mary wiped her hands on her towel and grabbed at the phone, flipping it open. "Sylvia!" she yelled. "Sylvia?" Then, "darn." She dropped the phone back onto her bunk. "I'll call her back after I'm dressed."

I sat there for a minute, looking up from the saffron rug and watching her struggle with her bra.

"Mary?" I said.

"Yeah?"

"I don't, um . . ."

"What?"

"Nothing."

"Don't worry, Peggy," Mary said. "Sylvia's harmless." She stomped her foot in frustration. "Can you hook this for me?"

I stood up and started to hook her bra in the back.

"Besides," she said. "It was kind of fun going to Mod today. It made me feel, I don't know. Bad. But good. Do you know what I mean?"

"No," I said. "I don't."

She picked up her comb and ran it through her hair again. Slow, careful strokes from her crown down past her shoulders.

After a moment, she stopped combing and just stared at herself in the mirror. She didn't move for what seemed like forever.

"Mary?" I said finally. "What is it? Mary?"

"Nothing," she said, quietly, softly, in that little voice of hers. "I'm just going to miss him, that's all." She looked up at Venus.

She put her comb away and finished getting dressed.

5

Because I was waiting for Mary,
I was late to work. Chef Jackie was on the phone when we arrived, and she didn't look too thrilled. "I don't want to hear that," she said. "I paid my bill, on time. Where is my delivery? It was supposed to be here *yesterday*." She snapped her fingers at me and pointed at a Post-it next to her laptop that said: garlic soup.

I hung up my coat, tied on an apron, swiped my knife against the honer, and started prepping the basket of garlic she'd left out for me. Mary slipped into the dining room to set tables.

"When do I need it? I needed it *yesterday*, Russell. I'm not happy." She slammed down the phone. "So much for the prosciutto-wrapped halibut that was the special we advertised this morning in the *Aspen Times*. We have no prosciutto. Brand-new freaking Berkel and no prosciutto." She walked over to the Berkel and patted the handle.

I shook my head. "That sucks."

"Yes, it does," she said. She sat down in her chair and tore her bandanna off her head. She shook out her hair. "We have thirty-two portions of halibut. Any ideas?"

"Oh, I don't know," I said, smashing a garlic clove. "I, um . . ." Of course I had a million ideas, but Chef Jackie probably had better ones.

"We'll just do it with bacon," she said. "Easy."

"That's a good idea," I said. But I knew better. The bacon we had was smoked at a farm up the road from us, and it had a very woody flavor, which would totally overpower the delicate halibut. And the texture of the bacon would be way too crunchy. "Except . . ."

"What?"

"Nothing."

"What?"

"I don't know. The bacon. It might be, I don't know. Too much."

"Yes," she said. "Too smoky. You're right. And too crispy."

Exactly.

"What about salami?" she said.

"Well," I said.

"What?"

"Spicy," I said.

"Hmm," she said. "Ham?"

"I don't know," I said.

She started pacing the floor. "Halibut. Halibut. Halibut."

"What if," I said. "Oh, nothing." I felt tongue-tied. It was one thing to come up with sabayon, which was just a condiment. It was another thing to come up with a dish at the eleventh hour that was easy and good enough to put on the menu that night.

"What?" she said. "What?"

"Well," I said. "What if, what if instead of finding a substitute for the prosciutto, why don't you make, like, a halibut *piccata*, you know with butter and capers and those Meyer lemons we got yesterday. We could serve a really delicate herbed hollandaise on the side."

"Piccata," Jackie replied, stroking her chin like she had a beard. "I never would have thought of that. I like it."

"We just got those salted capers in from BuonItalia; we could use those."

"I like it," she said. "Do we poach the halibut or bake it?"

"Pan roast it," I said. "So the skin gets crispy."

"Yes," said Jackie. "And we'll roast a half-sheet of lemons, too, to serve with each fillet. Roasted lemons are so beautiful on the plate, and their juice is so nice."

"Yum!" I said. And then, "Are you sure? I mean, it's just an idea. I'm sure you could think of something better."

"Peggy," said Jackie. "It's perfect. You saved the day."

Chef Jackie grabbed the specials board and started writing. "Halibut."

"Hey, Peg," she said. "Speak up more often, OK? You don't need permission."

6

I was hoping Jackie wouldn't
schedule Sylvia again after last night. The girl needed a
break. And more than that, the rest of us needed a break
from *her*.

But just before dinner service, in swept Sylvia. She
checked her coat with Edie (if left in the kitchen, she
explained, it would smell like garlic at the end of the night)
and rolled up the cuffs of her shirt, which was defiantly black.
"My white one was stained after last night," she said. "I had
to send it out for laundering."

Who uses words like *laundering*? I thought.

Chef Jackie didn't like it, but there wasn't much to be
done. And besides, she looked better in black.

Just as the first customers came in, Sylvia and I stood on opposite sides of the pass-through, she in the dining room pouring water glasses, me in the kitchen pounding pork cutlets for scallopini.

I noticed a chunk of waxy hair had broken free from her chignon. It flipped in front of her shoulder, and as she poured glasses, it was swinging in a slow arc from her cheek to her collarbone. I'd never seen her hair out of place. She made no move to fix it.

"Look," Sylvia said. "I know you saved me in here last night with the salads."

"Whatever," I said. I lay a pork cutlet on a sheet of wax paper, then lay another sheet on top. I whacked it with my mallet.

"I just wanted you to know that I know."

My first instinct was to ignore her, but then I thought about what Jackie said to me earlier in the kitchen. *Speak up more often. You don't need permission.*

"Are you thanking me?" I asked. "Or do you want something?" *Thwack.* With every stroke, the pork would splay out in the wax paper another quarter-inch. I had to get these cutlets down to a half-inch thick so Emma could batter and fry them to order.

"I don't want anything," she said. "Don't worry."

"Well, I want something," I said. *Whack*. "I want you to leave Mary alone."

"What do you mean?" Sylvia asked. "She doesn't seem to mind me. Besides, I'm helping her."

"She doesn't need your help," I said. "At all. She can take care of herself." *Whack*. "Besides, what about your own drama? Shouldn't you be paying attention to your *Howie*? Or do you not care if he's screwing some girl in Denver?"

"This, from *you*," Sylvia said. "You, who knew that your best friend's boyfriend was cheating with another girl, but didn't tell her. You, who let your best friend find out from *Amber*. You know what's best for Mary?" She sneered. "Hardly."

"I didn't know for a fact," I said. *Whack*.

Tempura-battered sweet potatoes with creamy dipping sauce. Lime-marinated chicken skewers with peanut sauce. Caramel iced tea.

"Oh, please," Sylvia said. "Either way, you should have told her, and you know it, *Peggy*."

"You're the one who set the whole thing up!" I shouted. "You gave her the gift card! You knew Amber would tell her!"

"So did you," Sylvia said. And she spun away to deliver the waters.

I kept pounding the cutlets into scallopini.

Baked cheese manicotti with spicy tomato sauce. Gyro sandwiches with tahini and hot sauce. Lemon pudding.

I was mad. I was mad because Sylvia was right. I should have told Mary. *Thwack*.

"Hey, Mary!" shouted Edie.

"She's in the bathroom," Sylvia said.

"No, I'm not," Mary said, emerging from behind the W door and drying her hands on a paper towel. "I'm right here."

"Stephen on line one," Edie said. "And can you please tell him to call you on your cell phone? I need this line for reservations."

"I'm not here," Mary said. She went back into the bathroom.

7

The halibut piccata was the fastest-

selling dish of the night.

Thursday

1

"Have you called Stephen back

yet?" I asked Mary as we shuffled into Western Civ.

"No," she said.

"Why?" I asked. "At this point, don't you want to find out what really happened?"

"I don't want to hear him lie to me."

Chef Jackie was pointing at her

laptop screen, excited. "I think you should go," she said.

She was at the Slow Food Web site. There was a posting on
the Web site that read:

Chef Daniela-Martina Verdun:

Dessert favorites for aspiring chefs

Demo: Strawberry fool, Sticky toffee pudding, Gubana

Friday, January 11, 1 P.M.

Ritz-Carlton Bachelor Gulch

Presented by the Enfants D'Escoffier, Vail Valley Chapter,

and Slow Food Vail Valley

$25 for members · $75 for non-members

"You have to go," Chef Jackie said.

"I can't," I said. "It's in Vail. That's an hour and a half away."

"So what?"

"I can't afford it." I studied the announcement for another minute. "What's *gubana*, anyway?"

"I don't know what gubana is. That's why I think you should go." Jackie tapped me on the shoulder and handed me a small stack of twenties. "You can be my spy."

"Chef, I . . ."

"Shh," she said. "Daniela Verdun is the best pastry chef in the state. She's always in the newspaper. I can't go because I have to be here to cook. You don't. Please go."

I actually knew who Daniela Verdun was. Mom took me to the restaurant where she cooks for my birthday last year, but it turned out she was on vacation, so the apple tart with the candle in it wasn't even made by her.

"You've more than earned it," she said, closing my hand around the bills.

"But it's tomorrow," I said. "I'm on the schedule."

"Shut up, Peg. You're going to Vail."

Friday

1

I never really invited her, but Mary came to the seminar with me. Not that I didn't want her to come, because of course I love hanging out with her, but, well, you know that feeling when you're really interested in something and someone else decides they want to come along and you're happy to have them, you guess, but this is your thing, not their thing, so it feels weird? It was like that. I mean, for me, getting to go to a seminar where Chef Daniela was teaching was a really big deal. For Mary, it was a way to kill a Friday afternoon and distract herself from everything else for awhile. And besides, seventy-five bucks didn't really register with her. She was rich.

But as soon as we left, I was glad she decided to come,

because it got Mary away from Sylvia, who was beyond toxic at this point. The air felt a lot cleaner without her around and Mary seemed more like herself. It also meant I didn't have to take the bus. Added bonus: Mary had a brand-new Audi with a killer sound system.

We left at eleven, which should have given us plenty of time to get there. It was one of those cloudy mountain days where the clouds seemed lower than the roof of Crawford Hall, one of those days where ten in the morning and three in the afternoon looked exactly the same, because the clouds were so thick you couldn't tell exactly where the sun was. There was snow in the air, but it wasn't coming from the clouds; instead, it was being swept up in spontaneous wind gusts like some kind of cosmic duster sweeping the roads.

The Roaring Fork Valley, surrounded by fourteen-thousand-foot peaks, was all but socked in. I couldn't see the tops of any of the peaks. But I could still feel the weight of them, not so much rising into the sky as leaning on the earth. Their heaviness made me groggy, and quiet.

Four-cheese pizza with caramelized onions and roasted garlic. Pan-fried noodles with crispy pork. Vanilla bean soufflé with cinnamon whipped cream.

At Glenwood Springs, where we picked up Interstate 70 for the last forty-five minutes to Vail, we stopped for

Starbucks. Mary got a latte, I stuck with regular coffee. But as soon as we got back in the car, I reclined my seat, and Mary put in the soundtrack to *Wicked*. It was even more cloudy in Glenwood Canyon. I'm not sure if I fell asleep or just zoned, but the drive flew by.

I thought I heard her phone ring during the drive, but she didn't answer. I suppose I could have dreamed it.

2

"Three-two-one," Mary said, pulling
up the drive and into the parking lot of the Ritz-Carlton
Bachelor Gulch. "It's showtime!"

"What are you, Ryan Seacrest?" I rubbed my eyes and
looked out the window. Gray skies, still. We pulled around
the side of the massive hotel. "This place is huge," I said. I
reached for my coffee, which wasn't there.

"Oops," Mary said. "You were asleep."

I checked my watch. One twenty. "We're late!" I yelled.

"We are?" she said, pulling into the valet station.

Mary tossed the keys to the valet guy, and we dashed inside.
A sign directed us to one of the ground-floor conference
rooms, one of those rooms that was probably a corporate

retreat banquet last night and will be a wedding tomorrow. About sixty chairs were set up in rows, all facing a "kitchen" up front, really a sort-of kitchen, set on a platform that had been wheeled in for the day. A mirror across the top of the set was angled so that from the audience, you could see whatever was going on at the countertop, which right now involved two big floppy sheets of dough. Two women with clipboards and glasses stood off to the side of the room.

Mary and I slipped into two padded folding chairs in the back row, a few seats in. I was next to a really tall girl.

Or at least, I thought she was tall. It was hard to tell since she was sitting down. She was wearing a charcoal cable-knit turtleneck sweater. A tiny silver cross hanging from a chain peeked over the turtleneck. Her hair was really short, like boy-short, a messy bed-head of dark brown roots and blond tips. She had really big hands. All of which screamed "volleyball player."

"Gubana," Chef Daniela was saying, "is a traditional dessert bread from Friuli, in the northeastern part of Italy. But it's more like a cake. A buttery cake-bread wrapped around a sweet fruit and nut and chocolate filling. Warm, in a bowl with a drizzle of heavy cream, on a snowy day—the best ever."

"Gubana," I said under my breath, pulling my notebook and pencil out of my bag.

"What'd we miss?" Mary had to lean across me to ask tall girl. "Anything good?"

"Strawberry fool."

That was fine, I figured. I knew how to make a strawberry fool. Berries, cream, mint, done. As long as we hadn't missed the gubana, which is what I was really here for anyway.

"I'm Flora," said tall girl. "I'm from Steamboat. Where are you guys from?"

"I'm Mary," Mary whispered. "This is Peggy." I looked over and nodded, but I didn't smile. I was actually trying to pay attention to Chef Daniela. "We're from Aspen," said Mary, waving her hand in front of me as if to point the direction there. "From Maroon Bells School."

"No way!" shout-whispered Flora. "Would you believe I'm heading to Aspen today, after the demo?"

"Shh!" I scolded. I hated being such a librarian but I actually wanted to hear about the gubana.

"It's really a very simple pastry to make," Chef Daniela was saying. "Simple, but not fast. My recipe is based on one from Mario Batali, but I doctored it up a little. It takes a little time, but it's so worth it." She was laying one sheet of pastry over another, and carefully lifting the edges of the bottom layer up over the top one. "Fold the bottom layer, the dry one, over the wet one like an envelope. Roll it out, and fold again.

And again. You have to do three rounds of this, with a half hour in the fridge between each round. That's it. Simple, like I said, but not fast. Luckily I have some here that's already gone through the fold-and-chill process."

The tall girl was still talking. "I'm thinking about moving to Aspen, actually. See if I can get a job at a bakery or something. I just graduated, a semester early, and my parents had a party for me, and halfway through the party I walked in on my boyfriend, Duane, I mean my ex-boyfriend, Duane, making out with some sophomore girl. On my couch. Can you believe it?"

"No way!" Mary whispered, leaning over me to get closer to Flora. "You walked in on him?"

What I really wanted to say was, "Can you shut the eff up already, because you have a big fat mouth and if you don't shut up, I'm going to stick something in it. Like my scarf." But I settled on "Shh. Please?" which I punctuated by pointing at Chef Daniela.

"So while your pastry is chilling, you can add your nuts and chocolates to the fruits you already have soaking in the wine. This will be the filling. Now, I know some of you aren't old enough to drink, but, well, you're not really drinking it, are you? You're just cooking with it." I noticed Chef Daniela look over at one of the clipboard-women, who shook her head. "But you can use pineapple juice, too. Just pour the fruit and the soaking liquid over the nuts and chocolate, stir it to combine, and carefully fold the egg whites in. Don't overwork it, or it will fall apart."

"It's fine, though. I'm dating this new guy now. Well, he's not that new, just new to me, well that's not true either because I used to date him a few years ago, but I haven't seen him for, like, months. He's a year older than me. And he just moved to Aspen. He's so cute, he has this cute little red beard. His name is Flip. Do you know him?"

Flip? I thought. *Can that really be someone's name?*

"No," Mary said. "We don't know him."

"Gently spoon the filling over the crust, and roll carefully. You don't want the crust to break. Not that it would be the worst thing in the world, but if you're going to all this trouble you might as well be careful. Once you've rolled in the filling, twist the gubana back on itself like a snail. Then, into the oven at 375 degrees for about forty-five minutes or so. It might take a couple practice runs at this altitude to get it exactly right."

"Have you ever made one of these before?" Flora said.

"I have. It was for a wedding. I work for a catering company. Well, more like I used to work for a catering company, before the owner died. Long story and yes, it had to do with a disgruntled client. Flip worked there for, like, one night, too, before he got called to join the ski patrol in Aspen. That's how we met."

"Ski patrol?" Mary said. "Stephen's on ski patrol."

"Stephen?" Flora said. "Who's that?"

I got up and moved to the front of the room so I could actually watch Chef Daniela.

3

"Did I hear you guys say you
were from Aspen?"

I was standing in line to meet Chef Daniela after the
demonstration. Mary and Flora were standing next to me,
chattering away. They weren't in line, really, they were just
there, talking about Aspen and Maroon Bells and Stephen
and Flip and who knows what else, when this other girl, this
really short girl with a mass of spiral curls that shot out from
her head in every direction, was peeking up at Flora (who
did turn out to be tall, very tall, even in the flat riding boots
she was wearing that looked almost exactly like Mary's) and
Mary. The girl was wearing a brown knit dress that went
right to the knee, a white cardigan, and ribbed navy tights.

With brown wing-tip oxfords. You know that girl in your elementary school who played the lead in *Annie*, then grew up to be the girl who always had her hand up in the front of the room? Her.

"Yeah," said Mary. "We're from Aspen. I'm Mary." She shook the girl's hand, then picked a lint ball off the girl's sweater. "This is Flora. And Peggy. Who are you?"

"Miriam," said the girl. "I'm on my way to Aspen. I'm starting school at Maroon Bells. I'm already a week late for the semester." She held out her hand to shake mine. "I'm a junior."

"Peggy," I said, shaking her hand but not taking my eyes off Chef Daniela.

"Hi." She smiled. Then, she looked around at each of us in turn. "Do you know where the bus station is?"

I looked over at Mary. I knew exactly how she would respond, so I started the countdown. *Three ... two ...*

"Do you need a ride to Aspen?" Mary asked.

"Really?" Miriam said. "I can pay." She smiled, what Granny would call a puppy smile, eager and hopeful.

"Do you have a lot of stuff?" I said, turning to face her. "Because we don't have a lot of room." I couldn't help being annoyed.

"No, my stuff is being shipped," Miriam said. "It should

be arriving at the school right about now. My mother timed it out. See, I've been in Vail all week skiing with the family. They left last night, but I stayed one extra night so my boyfriend could come spend the night with me. He was supposed to take me to Aspen today but he bailed. He forgot he had a test. He's in culinary school in Denver. He's a flake, but I love him." She shook her head and smiled. "Howie."

Howie? Wasn't that Sylvia's boyfriend's name?

I turned back to Chef Daniela, but she was gone.

4

Somehow, I got stuck in the back-
seat for the drive back to Aspen. Sure, Flora was about fourteen
feet tall, so it made sense for her to ride shotgun, but it still
sucked. I was cramped in the back with some girl in ribbed tights
who I didn't even know. She was small enough to cross her legs
and swing her oxford around in the air, which I hated her for.

*Angel hair pasta with garlic and olive oil. Carrot cake with
sweet cream frosting.*

Mary's phone rang twice on the drive back to Aspen.
The first time it rang, Mary yelled, "My butt's ringing!"
only I didn't laugh. She looked at the caller ID, sighed, and
switched her phone to vibrate. The second time, she turned
off her phone completely.

"Stephen?" Flora said.

"How'd you guess?" Mary asked, although it wasn't really a question.

I wanted to like Flora and Miriam, I really did. But my effing legs were in my effing chest, and it was effing uncomfortable. All I tried to do was come to Vail to learn something, and here I was stuck in the backseat for an hour-long drive with some girl whose tights annoyed me and who I had a sinking feeling was dating Sylvia's supposed boyfriend and was therefore about to cause even more drama in my already oversaturated social life. I wished she would just break up with him and get it over with.

Grilled ribeye with chipotle butter. Hot, salted French fries with garlic mayonnaise.

The clouds had lifted while we were in the demo, but the sun was starting to think about going down by the time we got on the road. While most of Glenwood Canyon was in shadows, every third turn or so we'd skim a patch of sunlight. I kept my sunglasses on the whole time.

"You want to know what I think, Mary?" Flora said. "I think you should call him back. He called four times in one day! No guy calls four times just to get his letter jacket back. Obviously he wants to apologize. He wants to clear things up. He wants you back."

Flora had no idea what she was talking about. How could she? She'd just met Mary like a couple hours ago. She'd never met Stephen. How could she be so sure? I didn't like it.

"What do you think, Miriam?" Flora said. She turned around and looked at us in the backseat. I couldn't believe she was asking her. Like preppy girl's opinion mattered.

"I don't know," Miriam said. "I don't understand boys. Howie doesn't even call me four times in a *week*. But I just thought all guys were like that. And besides, whenever I ask Howie where he's been or what he's been up to, he just gets mad at me."

Flora turned back to Mary. "He wants you. Call him. Listen, Mary, people will always tell you that there are more fish in the sea, but it's not true. There aren't that many good ones. If you find one you like, you have to fight for him."

"Forget it," Mary said, blowing her bangs out of her face. "I'm not calling. I have my pride."

Good, I thought. I don't know if I really agreed with her decision, but I was just glad she wasn't taking advice from Flora.

Warm gubana with heavy cream.

5

I wanted to stop at Reno on the
way back to Crawford Hall so I could give Chef Jackie a quick
report on the seminar while she was prepping for dinner
service. Mary agreed, and Flora and Miriam tagged along,
annoyingly.

We parked in the back and walked around the building to
the front door. There, arriving at the same time, was Sylvia,
all patent-leather chignon and wraparound shades and
jungle-red lips. She grabbed Mary's arm. "It's official," she
said, with a strange panic in her voice. "Howie is screwing
around on me."

"What do you mean," Mary said. She stepped in front of
Miriam, sort of blocking her from Sylvia's view. I wondered

if she meant to do it, or if it was some kind of subconscious protection mechanism that kicked in. I saw this episode of *Dr. Phil* recently that was all about subconscious mechanisms, where you do things that you don't even realize you're doing, for reasons you can't even articulate. But I wasn't sure who Mary was protecting, Miriam or Sylvia. All I knew was I didn't want to be there when Sylvia put the pieces together and realized that Howie's new fling was standing right in front of her.

"He's seeing someone, I'm sure of it," Sylvia said. "I just spoke to his roommate, and he hasn't been home in two days."

"That could mean anything, Sylvia," Mary said. "I mean, just because he's not getting back to you right away doesn't mean he's in Vail on some kind of romantic getaway."

Sylvia froze, halfway through opening the door to Reno, and locked her eyes on Mary's. "What do you mean, in Vail? How did you know he was in Vail? Did I say he was in Vail?"

Mary's eyes glazed over. "Um," Mary said. "Uh. He was? Wild guess, huh. I had no clue. Honestly. Vail?" She blinked, blank-faced.

Sylvia held steady, not moving, door half open, glaring into Mary. "Did you hear something?"

"I don't know what you mean," Mary said. She looked at

me, then at Flora, then at Miriam, then back at Sylvia, then at the floor. "Really."

Sylvia inhaled slowly, fluttering her feline eyes. "Liar," she said. "After all I've done for you."

Mary just looked at the floor.

"Tell Jackie I quit," Sylvia said, slamming the door to Reno. "Effective immediately."

"Gladly," I whispered as Sylvia stomped off into the twilight, stilettos clacking on the freshly shoveled sidewalk.

Miriam stepped out from behind Mary and said, to the air, "I didn't know he had a girlfriend." She blinked, slowly, once. "Honest."

Mary's phone rang. She looked at it, and stuffed it in her back pocket.

6

None of us were on the schedule that night, so Mary invited Flora and Miriam back to the dorm for grilled cheese sandwiches with Venus. She didn't ask me whether I would cook or not, she just invited them. And Edie, too. All of which meant I was standing at my desk in front of the George Foreman, looking out onto the street at the snow, falling in big round flakes, while everyone else sat in a circle below Venus.

"I don't know where Flip is," Flora said as she brushed grilled-cheese sandwich crumbs off her turtleneck. "I've called him twice already. I can't call again. He should call me." She took another bite. "This sandwich is amazing."

"It really is," Edie said. She tipped her head to one side to keep her goth bob out of her face.

"She puts butter on both sides," Mary said, pointing at me. I waved to Flora with my tongs and smiled, gritting my teeth. Just because she liked my food didn't mean she wasn't still getting on my effing nerves.

Persian honey cake with candied oranges.

"Maybe Flip thought you were coming to Aspen tomorrow," Mary said. She was leaning up against Venus's legs. Flora and Miriam were on pillows on the saffron carpeting. Flora was drinking a Red Bull.

Miriam stood up abruptly. "Where's the bathroom?" she said. "I really need to pee."

"I'll show you," I said, closing the George Foreman. "I have to go, too."

"I don't know. Do you think I should call him again?" Flora said, to all of us, I guess.

"Yes," Edie said. "Guys are stupid. They don't think to call you back. You have to call them if you ever want to get anywhere."

"Personally," Miriam said. "No. I don't think you should. Twice is enough." I opened the dorm room door to the hallway and held it open for her. "I would never call Howie more than twice without him calling me back." Miriam looked back into the room as she stepped out into the hallway. "I don't care if he's got a sautéing test the next morning or fourteen pounds of pasta to make or what. Howie needs to get on the kitchen phone and call me back."

I was looking back at Mary and Flora and Edie to see their reactions to Miriam's comments, but they were all staring straight past me, out into the hallway. Edie's mouth was hanging open. She made a little squeaking noise. Mary scrambled to her feet. Flora kept chewing. "What?" she said.

Without even turning around to see, I knew. And my stomach sank to my slippers.

"So it's you," Sylvia said. She stood in the hallway, in a belted black overcoat, hands on her hips, legs straight, shoulders back. She seemed taller than usual. She cinched her belt one notch tighter, driving home her skinniness.

"Excuse me?" Miriam held out her hand to shake Sylvia's. "I'm Miriam. Have we met?"

"I know who you are," Sylvia said. Or more like hissed.

"Well," Miriam said. "I'm new here." She stood firm, hand still outstretched. "I don't know who you are."

"Who I am?" Sylvia said. "I'm Howie's *girlfriend*. That's who I am." She cocked an eyebrow.

"Omigod," Edie said under her breath. "Omigod."

Miriam dropped her hand. "I'm afraid I don't know who

you are talking about. You see, my boyfriend lives in Denver. Excuse me."

Sylvia took a step forward, forcing Miriam into the doorway. "Oh, you know my Howie. And make no mistake, he's *my* Howie. No matter what you're doing with him."

"Excuse me," Miriam said again. She put her arms out to catch herself on the door frame. "I'd like to get past."

Sylvia stretched even taller, staring down at Miriam. She stretched her hands out to the sides. Miriam never took her eyes off Sylvia.

Suddenly, without warning, Miriam threw up her hands and tried to step past Sylvia, blocking Sylvia's outstretched hands with her forearms.

Sylvia swatted Miriam's hands away, keeping her trapped. "Don't touch me," she said. Growling. "Don't ever touch me."

"Then move," Miriam said. "Please." Her voice was stern. I couldn't believe how tough this preppy junior was being in the face of all this patent leather. She didn't seem intimidated at all. She put her hands back up to block Sylvia out of the way. She took a step.

Suddenly, Sylvia sprung at Miriam, pushing her against the wall and clawing at her curlicue hair. Miriam screamed, throwing her arms in front of her face to block Sylvia's grabbing hands. She threw out a leg, clocking Sylvia in the shin. Sylvia stumbled into Miriam, slapping wildly at her head, screaming, eyes bugging out.

Flora shouted and jumped up. I reached over and grabbed Miriam's waist with both hands, pulling her back into the room and out of Sylvia's reach, just as Mary came rushing to the doorway. She ran low and fast, like a football player, arms straight out in front. She dove at Sylvia's stomach and tackled her right to the floor. The two of them shot halfway across the hallway, landing in a loud, screaming, slapping pile.

"Stop it!" Mary yelled, jumping to her feet. "Sylvia, what is wrong with you?"

Sylvia stood up and smoothed her coat. "Get out of my way." Her voice was low, husky, angry. "Get. Out. Of. My. Way."

"Fine," Mary said, stepping aside.

"Backstabber," Sylvia said. "You knew all along."

"Give me a break, Sylvia," Mary said. "How could I know? We just met today." Mary ran her hands through her hair. "She didn't know Howie had a girlfriend."

Sylvia's mouth curved into a slow, sarcastic smile. "So you did know," she said. "I don't believe anything you say."

Mary stepped back into the doorway, nudging me into the room. She started to close the door, but Sylvia threw out an arm to hold the door open.

"Crystal's not the only one who Stephen hooked up with,

you know," she said. She cinched her belt, smoothed her hands along the sides of her head, and walked away. "Doesn't surprise me. It's not like he was getting any from *you*."

Mary closed the door, but it was too late to keep Sylvia's words from getting in. "Crystal's not the only one." They circled the room, bouncing off the corners and picking up speed, swirling tightly into a twister around Mary, blurring together and striking, knocking her onto her bunk. She sat there, feet hanging over the edge, staring at her socks.

Edie started feverishly tapping on her BlackBerry.

Mary's phone rang. She yanked it out of her back pocket, looked at it, and threw it against the bunk. "Stephen!"

"I really do have to pee," Miriam said. She scurried to the bathroom.

I started buttering bread for another round of grilled cheese sandwiches.

7

Somehow it didn't surprise me that
Flora and Miriam ended up spending the night in our room.

I'd been the first to call it quits, climbing up into my bunk
a little after midnight. "We'll try to keep it down," Flora had
said.

"It's OK," Mary said. "She can sleep through a tornado."

I really did intend to go to sleep, but I couldn't. I just lay
there, staring at Venus's head, which was glowing in the low
light of Mary's desk lamp. What must Venus have thought of
all of this? The girls kept chatting.

"Do you think Sylvia's crazy," Mary said. "Or what?"

"Maybe," Flora said. "But whatever she is, she's lost her
faith in love. She doesn't believe in it."

"I don't know if I do either," Mary said. "Not anymore."

"But it's the most important thing in the world," Flora said. "You know it is. You wouldn't have that huge picture of Venus in here if you didn't believe that."

"Aphrodite," Mary said.

"What?"

"Aphrodite."

"Whatever. Look, Mary, you have to call him back. You can't throw it away unless you know for sure. You haven't even talked to him, and it's just because you're being stubborn. You have to hear him out."

"But why?" Mary said. "So he can lie to me? If he cheated, he cheated. End of story."

"Mary. You're letting your heart break before you even talk to him."

"My heart's not breaking," Mary said.

"Yes it is, Mary. I can see it from here."

I would have thrown my pillow at Flora except for two things. One, I was supposed to be asleep. Two, she was right. Even with my eyes closed I could see Mary's heart breaking, too. And I cared about Mary's heart. I didn't want it to break.

But I didn't know how to stop it. And I was letting my own guilt get in the way.

I don't know what time Mary crawled into my bunk, but when her snoring woke me up, it was right in my ear. Flora and Miriam, I guessed, were crammed into Mary's bunk, and Mary was in mine.

My throat was stick dry. I thought about getting up to get a drink of water, but instead I just tried to fall back asleep. Once I got my breathing in rhythm with Mary's, it wasn't that hard.

Warm grits with butter and maple syrup. Four-cheese omelet with wild mushrooms. Vanilla bean pudding with dulce de leche.

1

When I woke up for real, I just opened my eyes. I didn't move. I just lay on my side and looked out the window across the room. The view wasn't much, just the alley behind Crawford that we shared with the back of Stephen's hotel, but it was soothing, especially in the morning light. Cloudy mornings don't explode into Aspen. They come slowly, drenching the town in a grayish pink glow before revealing the bracing white sun midmorning.

Three women emerged from the back door of the hotel. They were wearing maid's outfits. Two of them passed a cigarette back and forth. They laughed, and I wondered what they were laughing about. A coworker? A shared joke? A man?

It must have been colder outside than it looked, because they all went inside before they finished the cigarette.

Mary wasn't in my bunk anymore. She was standing in front of Venus, staring up at her. Flora and Miriam were already gone.

"Mary?" I said.

"She's so beautiful," Mary said.

"Yes."

"Maybe Flora is right," Mary said. "Maybe Jackie's right. Maybe I should give Stephen a chance to explain. Maybe I should give him a chance even if he did it."

"Mary," I said.

"Maybe love is bigger than those things. Even cheating. Maybe he loves me. And maybe he's the one." She reached up to touch Venus's face, like it was real. "Maybe I still love him."

I didn't say anything. For a few minutes, she stroked Venus's face and I watched her. Then she said, "I'm going to call him back."

It took me a minute to answer, but eventually I said, "OK."

2

She didn't call right away. First, we had breakfast.

I had two poached eggs on an English muffin, and Mary had granola. We got paper-cup coffees and took them out to the benches in front of Crawford. It was the first time I'd seen Mary drink the MBSG coffee. She was such a latte girl.

We approached the only bench that was in the sun. Mary said, "Hold this," and handed me her coffee. She took off her hat and used it to whisk away the snow that had fallen last night. Then, she took out her phone.

I sat down, holding both coffees, my hands shaking in the cold. Once she said she was going to call him, I knew I wouldn't think about anything else until it happened.

And now it was happening. Mary sat down, looked at her

phone, then looked at me. She plucked her coffee cup out of my hand, and took a long, deep sip, too long for such hot coffee. Then, she handed the cup back to me.

She sighed. "Here goes." She flipped open her phone, scrolled through the names, and landed on Stephen's. Staring straight ahead, she inhaled sharply and pressed "Send." I sat, stiffly still, holding two coffees.

"Hi, Stephen," she said. "It's me."

And then she said nothing for a long time. A very long time. I fought to keep from turning my head to look at her. If her face rose into a smile, I would worry. If her face fell into despair, I would worry more. It was lose-lose.

"I see," she said.

And then again, nothing for a very long time. I sipped my coffee, which was getting cold.

"OK, Stephen. Good-bye, Stephen." She lowered her phone into her lap from her ear without flipping it shut.

Mary sighed. After a moment, a very long moment, she closed her phone and held out her hand. I put her coffee cup in it. She raised it to her lips, but didn't sip.

"She's pregnant," Mary said. She sipped.

I stared straight ahead. I could hear laughter inside Crawford. It took me a moment to think of what to say, which was, "What?"

"Crystal is pregnant." She said it very lightly, casually, kind of like "I got an A minus on my psych exam," or "I got a new skirt."

"He said he is sorry. He says he loves me. That's all he said."

Mary smiled. She actually smiled. But it wasn't a real smile. It was a quiet, sad, lonely smile that made my stomach hurt. Granny never mentioned this one. "He can't leave her now, of course," she said. "That's it. It's over."

"Mary," I said.

"I'm fine. Look, I was fine before I met Stephen, and I'll be fine now, too. Right?"

That's when she started to cry. Loud, sudden sobs and stabbing gasps.

"Oh, my God. It hurts so much worse now," she gasped. "Oh, God." Her body collapsed forward, falling across her knees.

I dropped the coffee cups and lay my body across hers, to shield her. From everything.

I didn't bother saying everything was going to be OK.

3

Mary said she was going to the library. I don't know if she really wanted to go there, or if she just wanted to be alone and knew no one else would be there—not Stephen, not Crystal, not Sylvia.

I decided to go over to Reno and teach Chef Jackie how to make a gubana.

It was a good idea. Except on the way there, I stopped by the Timberlake for a coffee, to cancel out that icky cafeteria coffee I'd just suffered through.

Amber, as usual, was yakking on the phone. The coffee shop was packed, and she was the only one behind the bar, but she just ran through the customers one by one, chatting constantly.

"Yes, Reese and Jake were in here last week," she was saying. "And I heard Chris Brown was coming. I wonder if that means Rihanna will come." I'd made it to the front of the line so she nodded at me.

"Coffee," I said. "Small."

"Oh, please," she said into the phone while snapping the cap on my cup. "Hotel reservations are anything *but* confidential in this town." She mouthed, "Anything else?" and I mouthed back "Croissant, plain," which she grabbed out of the case and put onto a plate, still talking, "You know, I saw Matt Lauer night before last at D19. He looked so much older than he does on TV. Oh, and wait, did you hear? Yeah. The whole Stephen Haines thing. Yeah." Her voice went into a whisper as she made change from my five dollars. "She's pregnant. No, not that one, she's such a goody-goody, the other one! The one from the store."

So Amber knew, which meant everyone knew. I guess I shouldn't have been surprised, which was convenient because I *wasn't* surprised.

I paid for my latte and grabbed the last seat in the coffee shop, at the window bar right next to the cash register. I grabbed a stool and faced myself out toward the street, away from the crush of customers. I put my backpack on my lap and pulled my hoodie up over my head, cutting the rest of the customers out of my view, and me out of theirs. I bent over my croissant and started to pull it apart.

A few sips into my coffee, I heard Sylvia's unmistakable voice behind me. I knew she couldn't see me, deep as I was in my hoodie, but I bet her mouth wasn't two feet from my ears.

"Don't think you're so special just because you're wearing his jacket," she was saying. She sounded pissed. "You know he's only staying with you because you told him you're pregnant. He'll make sure you're taken care of, but he'll never marry you, Crystal. You can't seriously think someone like him would marry *you*?"

Holy crap. She was with Crystal. Since when do these two hang out? I couldn't believe it. Were they friends? No way. No, they must have had some reason. I wondered what kind of deal they'd struck, and why.

I was dying to turn around and see for sure that Crystal was wearing Stephen's jacket.

"Why don't you mind your own business," Crystal said. "Don't you have enough on your hands with Howie?"

"I'm finished with Howie," Sylvia said.

"That was quick," Crystal scoffed. "My phone's vibrating. Who is it?" I could hear her fumbling through her bag, dropping first a Kleenex packet, then a lip balm, then her phone onto the floor, still vibrating. It landed right at my feet. I looked down to see the lit caller ID: Flip

No way, I thought. No effing way. I didn't move. Sylvia's gloved hand slipped into my line of sight and grabbed away the phone.

"Flip?" Sylvia said. "Flip? Who is that?"

"Shut up," Crystal said. "Give me that." Then, "Hello? Hi."

Her voice switched quickly to the same purr it'd had in the fitting booth at Mod that day. "Hey, sexy. Can I call you back? OK. Yes, I'll see you later. Bye." I heard the phone clap shut.

"If Flip isn't Stephen's new nickname," Sylvia said, "then you're busted."

"Shut up," Crystal said. "I don't know what you're talking about."

"'Hey, sexy?' *Please*, Crystal. Who is he?"

"You can't prove anything."

"You're seeing someone named Flip. And you're pregnant. By Stephen. Or is it Flip's?"

"Shut up, Sylvia. It's none of your business."

"But I've decided it is my business," Sylvia began to whisper. "We are just one customer away from Amber right now, and I'm sure she'd have the entire valley saturated with this tidbit by lunchtime."

"Next," Amber barked.

"Whose baby is it, Crystal?"

"Next!"

"I'll have a cappuccino," said Crystal. She turned to Sylvia. "What do you want?"

"I'm not sure yet," Sylvia said. "But you can start with buying me a latte."

4

They say lightning never strikes twice, but within minutes, the second cell phone of the day slipped out of someone's purse and under my stool at the Timberlake. Only this time, it wasn't Crystal's.

This time, it was Sylvia's.

And this time, no one reached down to get it. In fact, it landed on a wadded up napkin and barely made a sound. I don't even think anyone noticed it fall.

I slowly lowered my backpack to the floor, to cover the phone. I'd wait for them to leave the shop before I pocketed it.

Camarones al Diablo. Chinese five-spice chicken with pomegranates and oranges. Apple charlotte with hand-cranked butter brickle ice cream.

5

Five minutes later, I had Sylvia's
cell phone in the innermost pocket of my parka, the most
secret place I could think of, on the inside of the waistband.

To be honest, I really didn't know what I would do with it.
It just seemed too perfect, dropping there, at my feet. It was
wrong. I knew that. But I took it.

I didn't set out to steal anyone's phone. And in fact, I
didn't steal it. Not exactly. It's more like I found it. And I was
keeping it safe for the time being. Until I decided to give it
back to her.

So I took it and put it in my coat and walked to the base
of the mountain. I felt like boarding, but it was Saturday, so
I'd have to pay, which meant forget it. But then I saw Carrie

from MBSG at the Shadow Mountain lift. She'd let me up free.

I ended up on the lift with three girls from Texas, who were all wearing earmuffs. Earmuffs just crack me up. I know they don't mess up your hair, or whatever, but they just look so, what's the word, stupid?

Black bean burritos with guacamole and salsa fresca. Sticky toffee pudding with heavy cream.

We'd almost reached the top of the lift when I felt my jacket vibrate.

Sylvia's phone.

Now what?

6

I hopped off the lift and boarded
over to Ruthie's, the lift that would take me to the top. This
time, thanks to some kid who wiped out on the loading
platform, I got the chair to myself.

I pulled off my gloves, hooked them together and stuck
them under my leg, then dug around my parka for the phone.
Within seconds, my hands were freezing, stiff. It was a sunny
day, but it was searingly cold. I could barely get my fingers
around the phone. I held it in one hand and blew on the other
to keep it warm.

It took only one button for the text to hit the screen. It
was from Crystal.

> **Not pregnant. Just testing the water. Ha ha.**
>
> **Boys so stupid. Don't tell anyone. Call.**

I stared at it, for, I don't know, ever? My fingers froze to numbness and the phone slipped out of my hands. It slid, quickly, across the bench of the chairlift. I lunged, but I missed it, leaning over just soon enough to watch it—and my gloves—spin into the air. The white phone disappeared into the snow. My gloves caught a thirty-foot pine tree branch and just hung there swaying like a Christmas ornament.

By the time I'd boarded down to the base, my fingers were blue.

7

"Are you crazy?" For the first time I could remember, Chef Jackie sounded truly angry.

"No, I'm not crazy," I said. "Yes, I am. I don't know. I shouldn't have taken the phone, I know. I shouldn't have read the text. I know. Believe me, I know. I don't know what happened. But I did it. I took it. And. Well."

I'd speed-spilled my guts to Chef Jackie over the last ten minutes, telling her in rapid, intricate detail the happenings of the previous week. I started crying about two words into the story, sobbing my way through the events until, dried up, I showed her my frozen hands, which were chapped and shaking and blue from the last run down the mountain.

"And then I came here."

Chef Jackie clasped my hands in hers. "If you want to be a chef," she said, "the hands come first. Don't ever do that again."

I tried to smile, but my face was too heavy. "How did this happen? How did I get here?"

"Because you are her friend," Chef Jackie said. "Because you care."

"So, now what?"

"I don't know," she said, picking up her knife. "I can't say. But I think I'd start with Mary."

8

I texted Mary: **Want latte?**

She texted back: **Meet where?**

I texted back: **Reno**

I was waiting by the front door when she walked up about
fifteen minutes later, stern-faced behind dark glasses and a
beanie. "Hi," she said.

"I have to talk to you," I said. And I started in. First I told
her about how I'd heard the gossip from Amber then how
I'd gone to Mod and overheard Crystal's conversation with
Stephen, and about how I didn't tell Mary about it because I
didn't know what to say. And then I told her about how I told
Sylvia to stay away from her. I told her that I thought she'd
been acting pretty crazy, like when she and Sylvia confronted

Crystal at Mod. And I told her how I hated that she'd made me sit in the backseat on the way home from Vail. And then I told her about seeing Sylvia and Crystal at the Timberlake, I told her about Crystal talking to Flip, I told her about Sylvia's phone, and I told her about the text. I told her that Crystal wasn't pregnant.

Mary didn't say a word the whole time I talked.

"I don't know what to say," I said. "I'm sorry, I guess. I should have done more. Or less. I don't know which."

"You should have told me," Mary said. "It would have been easier to hear it from you."

"I know," I said, forcing myself to look in her eyes. "I'm really sorry." I meant it.

"You should have told me, Peggy. That's all," Mary said. She turned and started down the sidewalk. "Didn't you say something about a latte?"

We walked to the Timberlake fast, very fast, in total silence. I had my head down, just watching my shoes crunch through the snow. I didn't know if Mary was mad at me, or if she was just mood swinging back to crazy, or whether she was just cold. I figured a head-down stance was best for now.

As we approached the front door, Mary suddenly stopped. "Well, what do we have here?" she said.

I looked up. There were only five people in the coffee

shop. Flora and Miriam, wearing matching sneakers, were facing each other at a central table, leafing through magazines. Amber was behind the counter, chatting on the phone. And at the milk-and-sugar station, with their backs to us but unmistakable in black stilettos and Stephen's letter jacket were Sylvia and Crystal.

I turned to Mary, who smiled and slipped her sunglasses back on. The last time she had that smile, it was with jungle-red lips. I liked it much better now.

She pulled open the door. "After you."

9

"I swear, I wish Stephen would stop calling me!" Mary said, loudly, as we approached the counter. She'd pretended not to see Crystal and Sylvia, keeping her sunglasses on, but was careful to be loud enough for them to hear. "I refuse to answer his calls. But I must have gotten like four or five messages from him today! Not to mention texts. I tell you, Peggy, it's pathetic. He's pathetic." We hit the counter. "One latte," she said. "And one coffee. She's buying." She pointed at me and smiled.

"I have to go," Amber said into the phone. I'd never seen her break off a call before. But she knew drama was afoot. She busied herself with Mary's latte.

I looked over at Crystal and Sylvia who had now turned to face us.

Mary pushed her sunglasses up onto her head. "Oh," she said. "Hello."

Crystal's phone rang. She smiled and flipped it open. "Stephen?" she said, or more like purred. "Hi, sexy." She leaned back on the counter, smiling. "Did you get us a room at the Durant tonight?" She was speaking a little too loud. Or *a lot* too loud. "We can pick out baby names."

Mary lunged at Crystal and grabbed the phone out of her hand. "Liar!" she shouted, or more like announced, to the coffee shop—and to Stephen, who was still on the line. "You're not pregnant, Crystal!" Mary waved the phone in the air, holding it just out of Crystal's reach, taunting her.

"Who do you think you are?" Crystal screeched, diving at Mary. "Give me that!"

Mary raced around behind the counter, where Amber was standing. "Give it up, Crystal!" she yelled, jumping up on the counter. "You're not pregnant. Are you? Isn't that what you told Sylvia?"

Crystal, sweating now, planted her feet, spun around, and glared at Sylvia. Breathing heavy, fast, she struggled to swallow and speak. "You?" she pointed at Sylvia. "You told! I told you not to tell!"

"I didn't know!" Sylvia shrieked.

"Liar!" Crystal yelled and lunged for the phone.

"Stephen!" she screamed. "Don't listen to them!"

Mary tossed Crystal's phone back to her. "Take it," she said. "You deserve each other."

Sylvia stood up and glared at Crystal. "You're not pregnant?"

"Don't act like you don't know," said Crystal.

"You're *not pregnant*?"

"So what?" Crystal said. "So what do you care, anyway? Now Stephen can just go back to Princess Mary over there. See if I care."

"You lied." Sylvia calmly opened her purse, which was hanging from her forearm. "Where is my phone?" She rummaged around in there, moving things around. "Where is my phone?" She started tossing purse-stuff on the counter: mascara, compact, gum, black licorice. "Where is my phone? I need to call Flip."

Flora, who'd been watching the drama, jumped out of her seat. "Flip?"

"That's right," Sylvia said. "Flip. The ski patrol guy Crystal is seeing on the side. He should know that he better use protection."

"Flip?" growled Flora. "*My Flip*?"

Suddenly, Flora sprung forward, hands straight out in front of her. She hit Crystal with both hands at once, knocking over two chairs and a two-top table before she landed directly on top of Crystal at Sylvia's knees, sending Sylvia skyward momentarily before crashing down on top of Flora. The three of them were a squealing, tangled mass of stilettos, riding boots, and Pumas.

Mary just stood there, watching in shock. She grabbed my hand and squeezed.

"Break it up!" yelled Amber. "Not in here!"

But Flora sprung up from the pack, and, enraged, grabbed a window barstool and swung it at the still-brawling Crystal and Sylvia. Sylvia's slicked hair had fallen out of its chignon. But Flora missed Crystal and instead sent the chair crashing through the floor-to-ceiling window and onto the sidewalk, littering the ground with huge shards of glass. A group of pedestrians screamed.

"Oh, my God," Amber shouted. She grabbed the phone. "Nine-one-one!"

The alarm set off by the broken window was swift and deafening, as a crowd of tourists—Russians, Argentines, and Texans—scurried over from all around to watch the fight, which didn't stop.

Mary and I stifled our giggles as Crystal and Sylvia continued to wrestle on the floor . . .

It took less than a minute for the cops to get there, but it took four of them to tear the girls apart.

10

"*Your butt's ringing,*" *I said to*
Mary as Sylvia and Crystal and Flora chattered to the cops.

"That's Stephen's ring," she said. She pulled her cell phone out of her back pocket and tossed it in the bushes. "I'm starving."

"Grilled cheese?"

"With butter on both sides."

11

"But I thought you and Stephen
would," I said, peeking into the George Foreman to see how
the grilled cheeses were coming. "I mean, I thought he . . .
I thought since she's not . . . I don't know what I thought."
I closed the cover. The sandwiches needed another minute.
"What about true love?" I asked.

She flopped down on the saffron floor and curled into a
ball at the feet of Venus. "I don't know."

"Have you ever seen her?" I asked.

"Who?"

"Her." I nodded at the poster. "Venus. I mean
Aphrodite."

"No. But maybe one day." Mary smiled.

I opened the George Foreman. The sandwiches were perfect. Golden-brown and glistening with butter. The Gouda and cheddar were just barely melting out the side.

I took the better-looking one, put it on a plate, and sliced it through the center, diagonally. I handed it to Mary.

Then I sat down on the pillow next to her.

"Thanks," she said.

"For the sandwich?" I asked.

My best friend, Mary, didn't say anything for a moment. Then she did.

"Yeah. For the *sandwich*. It's perfect."

"I don't know about perfect," I said. "But I'm working on it."

Mary smiled. For real.

Recipes *from* The Girls

PEGGY'S GRILLED CHEESE
SANDWICH

This is the best grilled cheese sandwich ever. Makes 1 sandwich.

Ingredients

- 2 slices freshly baked white bread (find the best baker in your neighborhood and buy it there)
- Plenty of butter
- A little mustard
- 2 slices smoked Gouda cheese
- 2 slices sharp cheddar cheese

Directions

1. Preheat your George Foreman Grill. Or, get a cast-iron pan nice and warm on the stovetop.

2. Butter both slices of bread on both sides with plenty of butter. Spread mustard on one side.

3. Place slices of cheese between bread slices, and press down, squishing the bread slices together with a spatula.

4. Place bread on George and close lid. Cook until bread has toasted on both sides and cheese begins to ooze out the sides. If using a cast-iron pan, place sandwich in pan, then place another heavy pan on top to squish it down. Cook until bread is brown, then flip and cook on the other side until cheese begins to ooze out the sides. Serve immediately.

CHEF JACKIE'S
ONION SOUP

If Reno was a real restaurant, this would be a bestseller.

Makes enough for 4 people.

Ingredients

- 2 tablespoons butter
- 2 tablespoons olive oil
- 4 large yellow onions, peeled and thinly sliced
- 4 garlic cloves, smashed and chopped
- 1 cup apple juice
- 1 tablespoon flour
- 6 cups beef stock or vegetable stock
- Salt and pepper
- 8 slices French baguette, lightly toasted
- 2 cups Gruyère cheese, grated
- A few leaves of parsley

Directions

1. Melt butter and olive oil in a large soup pot over medium heat on the stove. Add onions and cook, stirring every couple of minutes, until soft and barely brown. This will take about 20 minutes and it will smell really good. Add the garlic and stir for just 2 minutes. This will smell even better. Don't cook the garlic for any longer or it will burn and everything will taste bitter. Then pour the apple juice over the top and stir. Cook until the apple juice evaporates, about 15 minutes more. Stir in the flour until there are no lumps. Preheat the oven to 450 degrees.

2. Stir the stock into the onions. Bring to a low boil and simmer 30 minutes. Taste the soup and add salt and pepper until it tastes right.

3. Ladle the soup into 4 ovenproof soup bowls. Top each with two slices of baguette and sprinkle cheese over the top. Place soup bowls on a cookie sheet and slide them into the oven until the cheese is golden-brown and bubbly and crispy, about 5–10 minutes. Sprinkle with parsley and serve hot.

DANIELA-MARTINA VERDUN'S
WARM GUBANA WITH HEAVY CREAM

Simple, but not fast. Makes 1.

𝓘𝓷𝓰𝓻𝓮𝓭𝓲𝓮𝓷𝓽𝓼

- 1 cup walnuts, chopped roughly
- ½ cup hazelnuts, chopped roughly
- zest of 1 lemon
- zest of 1 orange
- ¼ cup candied lemon and orange peel, chopped together
- ¼ cup semi-sweet chocolate pieces, chopped roughly
- ¼ cup golden raisins, soaked for a few hours in strained pineapple juice
- 2 eggs separated, whites beaten until stiff
- ¼ cup sugar, plus 3 tablespoons
- 1 box frozen puff pastry

Directions

1. Preheat oven to 375 degrees. Lightly grease a large cookie sheet.

2. Get out your biggest mixing bowl and dump in the walnuts, hazelnuts, lemon zest, orange zest, candied peel, chocolate pieces, raisins, and soaking liquid. Stir it all together. Add the egg whites and ¼ cup sugar and, using a rubber spatula, carefully fold everything together with just 10 stirs. If you stir too much, you'll deflate the beaten eggs, and you'll have to start over.

3. Roll the pastry out to a 10-inch by 14-inch rectangle. Spread the nut mixture over the pastry, leaving about 2 inches uncovered at one end. Roll the pastry up from the bottom into a tube. Brush the end of the pastry with a little bit of water and press the pastry into itself to create a seal. Curl the tube into a spiral shape or circle. Beat the egg yolks and brush over the gubana. Sprinkle with 3 tablespoons of sugar.

4. Place on a cookie sheet and bake for about 45 minutes, until the crust is golden brown. Cool the sheet on wire rack for at least 10 minutes, then slice into pieces. Serve warm with a drizzle of heavy cream.

FLORA'S
STRAWBERRY FOOL

Easy enough for a fool to make, but nothing foolish about it.

Makes 4 fools.

Ingredients

- 1 pound fresh strawberries, stems removed
- ¼ cup sugar
- About 25 mint leaves, chopped very fine
- 2 cups heavy cream

Directions

1. Chop the strawberries into chunks. Stir sugar into strawberries. Add mint leaves. Place mixture in fridge for a couple of hours, stirring twice.

2. Whip cream until stiff. Stir strawberry mixture into cream. Scoop fool into parfait glasses, then place glasses into fridge for 2 hours or until stiff. Serve with gingersnaps.

PEGGY & JACKIE'S PAN-ROASTED HALIBUT PICCATA WITH BROILED LEMONS

Easy to make but fancy. Makes 4 servings.

Ingredients

- 1 tablespoon butter
- 1 clove of garlic, minced
- ½ cup fish stock or water
- juice of 1 lemon
- 2 tablespoons capers, drained
- 4 halibut fillets, about ⅓ pound each
- 1 tablespoon olive oil
- pinch kosher sea salt
- 2 lemons, halved
- ½ cup Parmesan cheese, grated

Directions

1. Preheat broiler in oven. Place oven rack about 3 inches from broiler flame.

2. Melt butter in saucepan over medium heat. Add garlic and stir for 2 minutes, no more. Add stock or water, lemon juice, and capers. Simmer over low heat.

3. Meanwhile, drizzle fish fillets with oil and sprinkle on both sides with salt. Place on ovenproof skillet or cookie sheet. Place lemon halves, cut side up, in skillet next to fish. Broil for three minutes. Flip fish over, sprinkle with Parmesan cheese, and broil 3–4 minutes longer, until cheese is browned and crispy. Place on individual plates and pour caper sauce over the top. Add half a lemon to each plate and serve.

Tucker Shaw is the author of *Confessions of a Back-up Dancer*, *Everything I Ate*, and *Flavor of the Week*. He lives in Denver, Colorado, where he works as a food editor at the *Denver Post*. He *never* gossips.